One Purpose

A NOVEL

MORGAN B. ANDRES

One Purpose
A NOVEL

Tate Publishing *& Enterprises*

One Purpose
Copyright © 2010 by Morgan B. Andres. All rights reserved.

No part of this publication may be reproduced, stored in a retrieval system or transmitted in any way by any means, electronic, mechanical, photocopy, recording or otherwise without the prior permission of the author except as provided by USA copyright law.

Scripture quotations are taken from the *Holy Bible, King James Version*, Cambridge, 1769. Used by permission. All rights reserved.

This novel is a work of fiction. Names, descriptions, entities, and incidents included in the story are products of the author's imagination. Any resemblance to actual persons, events, and entities is entirely coincidental.

The opinions expressed by the author are not necessarily those of Tate Publishing, LLC.

Published by Tate Publishing & Enterprises, LLC
127 E. Trade Center Terrace | Mustang, Oklahoma 73064 USA
1.888.361.9473 | www.tatepublishing.com

Tate Publishing is committed to excellence in the publishing industry. The company reflects the philosophy established by the founders, based on Psalm 68:11,
"The Lord gave the word and great was the company of those who published it."

Book design copyright © 2010 by Tate Publishing, LLC. All rights reserved.
Cover design by Kellie Southerland
Interior design by Stephanie Woloszyn

Published in the United States of America

ISBN: 978-1-61663-364-6
1. Fiction / Christian / Fantasy
10.06.01

To My Lord and Savior Jesus Christ, I thank you for the dream, time, will, tools, family, friends, and support, and for allowing me to get my dream published. Thank you, Tate Publishing! To Dad, Mom, Aaron, Trevor, and Austin, Grandpa Ron & Grandma Sherry, Pappa & Grama, Ms. Elsbrock, Mrs. Trahan, Ms. Driver, Mrs. Woolsey, Rachel, Katherine, Urmilla, Jessi S., Amanda, Maiya, Carissa, and Lindsey, thank you.

1

The sky was pitch black,

the moon shone on the glistening water, and a thick fog surrounded the village. A young, ten-year-old boy tossed and turned in his bed, haunted by a face that stared through his window at him as he tried to sleep. Just as he would begin to drift off, the nightmare returned, and the ice-cold eyes made him shiver in revulsion. He shut his eyes and tried to sleep without the image menacing his mind, but just couldn't make it leave. After tossing and turning for what seemed like an eternity, the boy finally gave up and slid out of bed. He nervously paced the room, but could not distract himself from the eerie thoughts, so he decided to face his fear and look out the window.

The boy stared blankly out the window, to try and clear his mind. As he stared into the darkness, his eyes grew heavy. He decided to crawl back in bed and try to go to sleep, but as he was walking away, he heard a thump on the wall behind him. The boy, scared that his nightmare had come true, slowly looked around his shoulder to see if something else was behind him. When he saw that nothing was there, he fully turned around and inspected the room. Everything was in its place, nothing had moved or fallen. It was then he heard another noise. The boy thought that it came from outside. Hesitating at first, he started walking cautiously toward the window. When he reached for the windowsill and looked out, all he saw was a thick white fog in front of him, nothing else. Just as he was about to turn away, two gleaming red eyes jumped in front of him from outside the window. The boy gasped and moved backwards tripping over his feet, flying to the floor. Too scared to move, the boy just glared into the red eyes. As he studied the eyes, he noticed that something was odd and knew that those weren't like anything he had seen before, not even an animal's. Finally the eyes seeped back into the white fog.

When the boy broke out of his gaze, he realized what he had just seen. He jumped to his feet and ran for the front door. He was torn between feelings of fear and curiosity, but curiosity won. Going outside was the only option.

Within the first few steps the boy took, shivers ran down his spine; they slowed him down but didn't stop him. After a moment, the boy didn't know where he was going, so he stuck his arms out and used them as guides. He walked around and around for a couple minutes until he came across something that felt rather bumpy and rough. The boy figured that it was some kind of wall and kept feeling around to see if there was a door, but when he did, he felt the outline of an arm.

While he felt around, he didn't notice that something was coming up behind him. Once the boy turned around, he saw a tall, dark green being standing only a hair away. His heart filled to the brim with fright, and he didn't know what to do; he just stood there, full of fear. The being in front of him examined him; it tilted its head, and the boy saw how the tip of its head curved down. The being pulled up its arm; the boy's eyes grew to the size of golf balls. Its fingers were like french fries, its nails grew long and straight, and the being had the same gleaming red eyes that he had seen in his window.

It slowly reached out and grabbed the boy by the chin; turning his head to the left, studying him. Then the being turned the boy's chin to the right and did the same thing. The boy shut his eyes tightly and hoped that whatever the being was going to do would be over soon. When he felt the dry, bumpy hand let go of his chin, the boy peeked through one of his eyes, in doing so he felt what seemed to be a knife scraping down the side of his arm, taking a long, thin piece of his skin. The boy held back his scream and took in the pain as the being dissipated into the air.

Once it was all over, the boy yelled in agony and pain as he tightly gripped his arm, feeling the blood come rushing out, he ran through the mist back the way he came.

The boy shot through the open door. Breathing heavily he fell to his knees trying to hold back his tears as he let go of his arm to check the status of his injury. Blood shot out of the long cut and spewed everywhere; the boy didn't know what do. He stood up gripping his arm and ran to his mom and dad's room. The boy busted the door open and screamed, "Mom, Dad, help!" But there was no answer to his cry. He then thought to himself about where his parents could be as he gripped his arm tightly. *Think, Brandon, think. Where could they be if they're not in their room?* He couldn't think of any place they would be, so he checked everywhere: the living room, the kitchen, the dining room, the bathrooms, the extra rooms, and even the dark basement. His parents were nowhere to be seen.

Brandon paced around in a circle, thinking aloud of what could have happened to his parents. "Where could they be? Surely they wouldn't leave the house while I was sleeping? But that's the only solution." Brandon eventually drifted to the subject of the monsters outside; maybe they did something to his parents. "Could something like that kill someone? I wouldn't think so, I mean...it was just...just nails...that's all; nails can always cut someone...Kami's have cut me before. Maybe this is all my imagination? But what if it isn't?" After standing for five minutes, Brandon had become tired and sat down. But within ten minutes of fighting to stay awake, he had fallen asleep. The time went from two to six o'clock in a flash.

Awakening to the sun slipping through the wooden blinds, Brandon opened the front door to look outside. He saw that the fog had thinned. Brandon's heart pounded in his chest as he sat there and prayed, "Dear God, please let my parents be okay, wherever they are, please." He started to tear up and continued, "Please, God, please, oh please let them be okay." Brandon slowly stood up. Wiping the tears from his cheeks and ran to his parents' bedroom. Brandon looked in the bed, but saw no one. He looked around their room shouting, "Mom, Dad, where are you?" There was no answer. Brandon thought the worst and took off outside.

Once he stepped outside, Brandon looked toward the village square and saw a group of people standing in a circle. He was convinced his parents were in the crowd warning the villagers about the monsters he had seen last night, Brandon ran shoving people to the side, with joy on his face, shouting, "Mom, Dad!" But once he witnessed what everyone was looking at, his happy face disappeared, and he broke down into tears.

In the center of the crowd were his parents, lying on the ground. Their throats had been slit. The people knew that the two were his parents. They tried to keep him away and calm him down, but all Brandon did was viciously fight back to get near them and cry.

2

The eyes of an eighteen-year-old boy opened with fear, his heart beating excessively in his chest and cold sweat pouring down his face. He sat up and slid his feet off to the side. "Not again. How long until these memories go away!" he whispered to himself as he put his head into his hands.

Brandon lived in a lost forest with his best friend Kami; they had remained there since the age of ten. Though they were ten-year-olds, they had learned what to do to survive in almost any circumstance since the village they had grown up together in was out in the middle of nowhere and the people had to work to survive.

Brandon had built a tree house out of logs, in-between two close trees. Kami made their beds out of smaller logs, which were covered with leaves to make it a little roomier. They used the only clothes they had, the clothes they wore when they were *taken* from their home.

The weight-balanced elevator to get up and down the tree house worked with a very heavy rock tied to a couple of vines which connected to the bamboo elevator. The elevator stayed up high, but when they needed it, all they would do was put the rock in-between two close branches, which were up high, and the bamboo would come down. Once on the elevator, they would knock down the rock with a big stick and the weight of the rock would outweigh the teens, sending them up to their house.

Brandon finally stood up and paced around the room, even through his clothes, the well defined muscles of this eighteen-year-old man were evident. His straight, short, light brown hair and solid brown eyes showed he wasn't scared of anything. He had a natural build; broad shoulders, a six-pack from all the work he had to do, and a rectangular face that just looked tough. When he staggered out onto the mini balcony around the tree house, he glanced down and saw Kami standing below.

Looking up, Kami waved then signaled for him to come down. Brandon headed for the elevator.

Once he stepped out, Kami jogged up to him and asked, "Sleep well?"

"Naw, I had that…nightmare again last night. You know, the one that makes me relive the moment when I lost my parents."

"Ouch. That isn't cool."

The two started strolling around the forest while talking and picking up sticks for the nightly fire. "Did *you* sleep nice?" asked Brandon.

"Yea, you could say that, except I kept waking up in the middle of the night, but that's all," Kami replied. She looked at him and cracked a grin then bent back down to pick up a stick.

"Do you remember those beings that made the blurry spot that we fell into?" questioned Brandon.

"Sure, they were those dark green creatures that had

the longest fingers you would ever see, with even longer fingernails!" stated Kami "The thing that really bothered me was the way their toes and head curved down."

"They were also in my nightmare," said Brandon in a soft tone.

"But do you remember how we ended up in this forest?" asked Kami as if they were competing to see who remembered the most.

"Well, those beings had you and I backed into a corner in the back alley when this blur-type thing sucked us in and landed us here," replied Brandon.

"Yep." Kami looked up and smiled.

Brandon and Kami had been friends since forever; something about her always made him want to smile, even in the worst situations. Maybe it was how her face had an oval shape to it, allowing her glittering green eyes to be positioned just above her high cheekbones and below her light eyebrows. Or it was how her short light brown hair flowed with the damp forest breeze. Perhaps it was how her small smile could be so powerful.

They were now collecting different things like food, water, and wood to build things they needed or that they wanted. Their tree house was located in the middle of an orchard of fruit trees and had a beautiful stream flowing close by. Brandon had wandered off to garner logs for their home, while Kami went to harvest some fruit and water as a part of their daily routine.

When the sun set to get some sleep and the moon rose from its nap Brandon and Kami were sitting by the fire, warming themselves from the cold damp forest weather. The two cuddled up next to each other, Kami looked up at Brandon, who was taller and asked, "So what did you build today?"

"Uh, I built two pantry like things, one for each of our rooms, so you could just store the food there instead of all over."

"That's awesome,"

"Oh, and I also made *you* this." Brandon let go of Kami and leaned down. When he came up, he held something behind his back. "Okay, you have to close your eyes." Kami did what she was told and closed her eyes, and then Brandon told her to open. When she did, she saw that he was holding a bamboo jewelry box. Kami gasped with shock.

"Oh my gosh, Brandon, this is so beautiful! Thank you. Thank you so much!" Brandon took her hand and gave her the box.

"Open it," he insisted. Kami gazed into his eyes and smiled, then opened the box. Inside, lying on the bottom was a necklace. Kami picked it up and held it in the air. The strand that was supposed to go around the neck was green and looked like it was skinned; the charm hanging down was a tiger tooth.

"Brandon, this is gorgeous. How did you make these?"

"I made the box out of bamboo and the necklace out of some vine and a tiger's tooth."

"Wow, where did you get the tooth?"

"From the tiger I killed about three months ago."

"What! You killed a tiger?"

"Yea, that's why we had all that meat."

"You told me that came from—wait, you never ever told me where that came from!"

Brandon laughed under his breath then smiled.

"Surprise!" Brandon stood up and walked around Kami. "Here. Let me see the necklace." Kami gave it to him, and she turned around to face the opposite way as Brandon laid the necklace around her neck. Once it was on, Brandon sat back down on the log.

Kami touched the tooth and smiled. "Thank you so much. This is the best gift ever." She leaned over and gave him a hug.

The two didn't stay up too late that night, but instead each went to bed so they could get an early start in the morning. When they woke up, they started on their daily chores. Kami still wore the necklace that Brandon had given her.

It went from dawn to dusk in a flash. Kami and Brandon were sitting around the nightly fire as usual talking about what it would have been like if the beings wouldn't have came. "Yea, I say that my life would have been a lot better if they hadn't come and killed my parents or taken us away from the village," explained Brandon.

"I don't know. I kinda like being out here sometimes because it just seems like everything is much calmer, and no one tells us what to do or how to do it," stated Kami. Brandon put his arm over Kami's shoulder, and she laid on it. They both just sat there absorbing the warmth of the fire.

When they suddenly heard a ruffle in the trees above them, Kami jumped, skimming through the trees around them, gripping Brandon's arm. "What was that?" questioned Kami.

Brandon calmly glanced around in all directions but couldn't make out anything. "It was probably the wind."

They went back to talking and staying warm by

the fire, when they heard it again except this time, all around them. For a second it seemed that it *was* the wind, still whistling through the trees, but when little gleaming red eyes popped up all over, it changed their theory. They were surrounded by swarms of red eyes, shining all around them. Brandon stood up, holding Kami's hand, and whispered, "When they start climbing down the trees, we run on the count of three straight through those trees." He pointed low at the spot. "I don't know what it is, but it's best to run." Brandon kept his eyes peeled for anything and everything, but as more ruffles started, he knew they were coming down. "One, two, three!" They sprang through and into the rest of the forest.

Both Brandon and Kami ran as fast as they could, scrambling, trying hard to keep their balance, run, and dodge all the branches. Though they were ahead, they could see a sea of red eyes gaining on them. Dodging all the branches that were in the way and jumping over broken wood, nothing would stop or slow down the two. Brandon looked back to see how far ahead they were, but when he did he saw that the beings were gone. Not one pair of eyes was behind them. He surveyed the trees confusedly and quit running. Kami did the same, still gripping Brandon's hand and inquired nervously, "What just happened?"

As she turned around, Brandon still looking around in all directions stopped to answer. "I don't know. This didn't happen..." He blanked out in the middle of his sentence. Kami wondered what was wrong, until she saw Brandon look up. In all the trees that surrounded them, they could make out some unusual figures above. Though their bodies blended in with the leaves, their red eyes shone brightly, yet again.

Kami and Brandon's heartbeats grew louder and quicker. Sweat dripped off their faces and ran down the back of their necks. A shock of fear and worry skidded down their spines.

They knew that the beings would never leave until they accomplished the task they were here to do. The two went back to back as the beings climbed down from the trees and surrounded them. This time there was a complete guard all around them and truly no place to run.

All they could do was watch as more and more beings showed up. Brandon looked over his shoulder and whispered, "Kami, do you remember there being this many of these creatures?"

Kami looked back at him over her shoulder and replied in terror, "No, I don't. Do you think they're showing up from those blurs?"

"I don't know, but if they are, then there is a small chance that we could possibly escape this through one of those like last time." Kami nodded her head and looked back at the beings, and so did Brandon.

They stared at the beings for several more minutes, waiting for them to attack or for a blur to show up, when just a few yards in front of Kami, a blur suddenly appeared. Kami started to run for it and yelled at Brandon, "A blur! Come on!" Brandon turned around and started to run for it; he saw that Kami had jumped in, so he ran faster. He suddenly felt a slight pinch on the back of his neck, and his legs went numb in seconds as he tripped and fell to the ground an inch away from the blur. His sight blurred, and soon his mind went black.

3

The sidewalk started to blur,

shooting Kami out; she hit her head and flung to the side. She lay still for a second then sat up slowly, trying to ignore the pain inflicted on her back and head. She rubbed her eyes to get her sight back, but when she did, she saw that Brandon wasn't there. Instead she saw four figures standing in front of her. They were all still a little fuzzy. Kami staggered up, holding her back and head along the way, and queried, "Where…? Where am I? And where's Brandon?"

One of the guys stepped forward and answered, "You're in Andren, the city. And who is Brandon?"

Kami looked up at him and replied, "You know, the guy who…"

She viewed behind her. Seeing nothing, she started to panic. "No! Where is he? He must have made it through the blur too!" All four of the figures' faces lit up, and another guy, whose voice was deeper, asked, "Blur? You mean the ones that the Seekers use?"

A confused look crossed Kami's face. "See-Seekers? Ah, my head and back." Kami placed her hands on her head and back as she stumbled around trying to regain balance. Her head throbbing with pain, Kami lost the little balance she had and started to fall, but the guy who first spoke leaned over and caught her in his arms. He picked her up and continued to walk with the others.

❧❧

As Kami's eyes opened, things still seemed a little blurry, and standing in front of her was Brandon smiling, wearing the same clothes and everything. He started to speak softly, "Are you okay?" Kami tried to smile and replied, "Brandon, is that really you?"

"Brandon? Who is this guy you keep talking about?" questioned the mystery person. Her eyes cleared up. Brandon disappeared to reveal the guy that first spoke. "My name is Johnny, but you can call me Jon. And who are you?"

Kami rubbed her eyes to see a guy sitting in a chair beside her bed. He reminded her of a friend of her Dad's that was always pulling pranks and cracking jokes. She examined Jon before answering. "Kami," she gave her name first then continued. "Brandon is the guy I was with in the forest. Now where am I?"

Jon leaned back and cocked his head with confusion. "Huh, forest? No, you're at a hospital, and there are some people that want to see you!" Jon moved, and standing behind him were two girls, and behind them was one last guy leaning up against the doorway with his hands shoved into his pockets.

Jon walked between the two girls and pointed to the blonde with shining blue eyes and dimples. "This is

Rachel." Then he pointed to the other girl. "And this is Katherine."

Katherine had brown hair and hazel eyes. Even though the girls were very petite, Kami thought they looked athletic; she could tell they were both in great shape.

Jon walked over to the last guy who looked almost scary the way his black shaggy hair hung over his dark brown eyes. "And last but not least, this is Zak!"

Kami sat up and nervously, almost terrified, and said "Hi, I'm Kami."

Zak leaped off the doorway, walked over to a chair beside her bed and sat backwards in it, facing her. He spoke in a deep voice, being very straightforward. "So you know what Seekers are, right? The dark green, red-eyed, freak-shaped things?"

"Yea?" Kami answered back still confused and scared, then continued. "They attacked me and this other guy named Brandon twice, once at our village. They killed his parents during that attack, and the blur took us away to this forest, and there they attacked us again. Another blur appeared when they had us surrounded; I reached through, but I don't know if he did."

Zak looked at her and replied, "Okay, well, I can have a city search going on in like two minutes to see if he's in our city or in the perimeters around. What does he look like?"

Kami replied, "He has straight brown hair, brown eyes, a natural build with a six-pack and a tough-guy-looking face."

"All right, that's all I need. Every time you go out, make sure you're with someone. They'll probably attack again. Let me know if you remember anything else."

Zak stepped up over the chair and walked toward the door when Kami hollered, still nervous. "Thank you!" Zak just kept walking.

Everyone else kinda stood there until Katherine spoke as Rachel and Jon walked out. "He scares you, doesn't he?"

"No…" replied Kami, trying not to admit it.

"It's all right." Katherine laughed. "At first that's how most people feel, but after a while the feeling goes away and you get used to it."

Kami giggled then asked, "So what's a city? And a hospital?"

Katherine sat in the chair. "A city is a bigger and more advanced home; you lived in a village, which is smaller and less advanced. A hospital is a place where you come if you're sick or injured, and doctors are the ones that make you feel better," explained Katherine, trying to break the information down for easy understanding. Kami still looked confused, but it made sense.

"Okay. That's cool."

Katherine smiled and said, "When you're able to leave, Rachel and I will show you around." She paused a moment then continued eagerly, as if she wanted an adventure. "And maybe by that time, if we don't find Brandon, we can go out to the other cities and countries to look for him."

"That sounds awesome! But you guys don't need too. I can look for him myself," she replied back politely, not wanting to be a bother.

A few days passed, and Kami recovered from her minor head and back injury and had already left the hospital. Like Katherine said, she and Rachel were showing Kami around.

"That's where all four of us live." Rachel pointed out as they walked past a little house. It was a dark-bricked house, one story, but it was pretty wide.

"And soon, if you want to, you'll live there too since you're not from around here!" Katherine added. The three wandered around the huge city, seeing all the nice homes, work buildings, and restaurants.

As they finally finished the tour, the sun was setting, and they were walking home. They had just a few blocks till their house. "So why are there cities?" asked Kami.

"What do you mean?" questioned Rachel.

"Well, I lived in a village, and you live in a city. Why are there two different things instead of one big city or village?"

"Oh," responded Rachel, understanding what Kami meant. "Well, a long time ago when we were just learning about technology and scientists were introducing it to the people, a large group of citizens started protesting in anger because they thought that having this kind of technology was going to corrupt the minds of people and they would become too dependent on it. But another group thought the opposite. They believed that people *should* start learning more about and using technology to expand their lifestyle and better their way of life. These two groups argued and argued for many years over this, until one very important guy in our history came out from the crowd and came up with a compromise. His name was Drew Clayooks. He became very famous for settling the argument. This compromise benefited everyone because each group received what they wanted. The people who wanted things to stay the same now live on the outskirts of the country, and the people who wanted change live in the middle of the country."

"So what are your opinions on the conflict?"

"Well, I believe that we should have moved on with the technology because now look, we can help many more people with disease, help better communication and transportation, and help set a future for the children."

"Well, mine," started Katherine, "I think both sides had a point. Those who wanted things to stay the same had known that way for a long time and feared the outcome of what technology would do to people. As for the other group, I think that trying something that could have potentially helped us develop was also a good point."

Kami looked up into the sky, thinking about what her choice would be. "I don't really have an opinion. I'd just go with whatever."

It was getting darker, the sun had completely vanished, and the night sky was settling in. The three were just about home when suddenly the road in front of them started to blur up. Kami looked carefully at the spot hoping that the one coming out was Brandon. Katherine and Rachel didn't know what to think, so they backed away, pulling Kami along with them. When the blur cleared up, six Seekers leaped out and started charging after Kami.

All the Seekers reached halfway to Kami, but at that point, five stopped and waited to see what would happen. When the lead Seeker reached about a foot away,

Katherine and Rachel reached into their small bags and jammed their weapons into the heart of the Seeker. They each slid their weapons out from the side of the Seeker, and it slowly dissipated into the air.

Katherine's weapons were daggers that could be thrown for long range or just jabbed into the enemy for up close. As for Rachel, she had a long spear that shot out on both sides or on just one at will, by the push of a button.

Five Seekers still remained. They only stood there, perhaps waiting for the opportune moment to strike. Or maybe they were waiting for Katherine and Rachel to step aside so that they could capture Kami. Katherine and Rachel kept their guard up while Kami stood in the back scared to death of the Seekers that stood in front of her. The Seekers limped, like their back legs were broken, forward a few steps then stopped. This was very odd behavior for the Seekers; normally they would show up and attack at the first glimpse of their enemy.

Suddenly four of the Seekers sprang to each side, two on one and two on the other. Katherine and Rachel turned to opposite sides and attacked the two Seekers that came near them. Little did they notice that the last Seeker was sprinting and limping right through the middle path toward Kami.

"Guys... uh, there's one last one, and it's... coming this way!" screamed Kami as she started to run. Katherine turned to look at Kami and saw the Seeker start sprinting after her; she grabbed the Seeker in front of her and threw it over her head and onto the ground, then started chasing after Kami. Rachel then stabbed the Seeker she was battling and knocked it to the ground.

Both Katherine and Rachel were gaining on the

Seeker. As they reached close enough, they looked at each other and winked, then Rachel ran up ahead a little and knelt down, getting her hands ready for Katherine. Once Katherine reached Rachel, she jumped onto Rachel's hands and leaped off. Rachel then pushed what she could on Katherine to give an extra boost. Katherine flew through the air, when she came above the Seeker. She reached into the bag she had on her side and grabbed four knives and threw them all, nailing the Seeker in a line on the back. Once the knives struck the Seeker, it stopped and dissipated slowly into the air while the knives dropped to the ground completely unharmed and perfectly clean.

Katherine dropped out of the air and landed on both of her feet, then dropped to a knee after losing her balance. Rachel caught up and helped Katherine stand while Kami noticed that the Seeker was gone and stopped running.

Katherine went and picked up her knives as Rachel turned around; they both put away their weapons, and Kami looked at them with astonishment. "Wow! I can't believe you can kill them!"

"Sure you can! Why wouldn't you be able to?" Rachel giggled as she asked.

"I don't know, I've just run from them for so long that I just thought they were invincible!" explained Kami with a laugh as she shrugged.

"Well, around here, dusk or later is when they mostly come out, so that's why we carry these," explained Katherine.

"Guess that means that Zak and Jon have weapons too, right?" asked Kami.

"Yep, Zak has a long, black blade, and Jon has a creshen, which is a blade that curves around your elbow when it's held, and the edge of the blade has spikes on it. His weapon is so different, 'cause it has this button on the side that sucks the spikes into the main blade then the main blade is sucked into the handle," answered Rachel.

"Hey, we need to get home before more Seekers come out," warned Katherine.

On the jog back to the house, Rachel noticed the vine necklace Kami had on, around her neck. "What's up with the necklace?" Kami looked at it and held it in her hand.

"Oh, Brandon made this for me when we were in the forest. He always built things to add on to our house, and...oh my gosh!" Kami stopped running, she covered her mouth, kneeling down, her voice filled with sadness. "The...the box! The jewelry box! No!" Her eyes started to tear up. Rachel knelt down beside her.

"What? What are you talking about?"

"The jewelry box Brandon made me! I...I don't have it! I left it behind when the Seekers were following us!"

Katherine looked at Kami. "I'm sorry that you lost it, but you made the right choice...your life is a million times more important."

"I know, but still that box...at least I still have the necklace," she whispered to herself as a tear ran down her cheek. "He made this out of a vine and a tiger tooth." She giggled a little remembering how he tried to get off the subject of him not telling her about the tiger. "He surprised me with it, and he also made a bamboo jewelry box for the necklace to go in."

Both Katherine and Rachel said, "That's so sweet!"

"I know, and he's... we better get going."

Kami stood back up and continued jogging with the other two behind.

※

"You're going to get a weapon to defend yourself with, okay?" Rachel said as she went into a closet to grab one.

"Okay, but what is it going to be?" asked Kami. When Rachel came out of the closet, she was holding a whiplike thing made of chains with spikes all over it.

"So what do you think?" asked Rachel as she handed it to Kami.

"That is so awesome!" Kami stepped back and swung it around a little.

"There's a button on the side, and when you press it, the entire whip will be pulled into the main handle."

"Wow, thanks. This is amazing!" exclaimed Kami when she heard that her name was being called.

"Kami, get over here!" yelled a voice from across the house.

Kami shouted back, "Okay, I'll be there in a second!" She hit the button, and the chain flew into the handle.

Just before Kami was about to leave, Rachel grabbed a small light green bag and called to Kami, "Wait." Kami turned around and Rachel tossed her the bag and continued, "Put your weapon in that, or if you want, you can put it in a case and carry it around like what the guys do—either way." Kami placed the weapon in the new bag thanking Rachel as she ran up the stairs, then headed to the room from which her name was being called.

Once she was there, she saw that Zak and Jon were

sitting on a table off to the side, leaving room to see the big TV in front of her. On the screen showed the words, *City search for male around the age of eighteen, straight brown hair, brown eyes, natural build with a six-pack, tough-guy face...*

Kami looked at the words and asked Zak, "So if we press enter, then it will show every guy in this city with those qualifications?"

Zak nodded and Jon spoke up eagerly, "Well, go on, press enter!" Kami looked at the two guys and walked forward to the keyboard and pressed enter. When she looked up onto the screen again, the words were *Searching... searching... searching...* until the results came up. Pictures of every guy in the city with those descriptions showed, Kami scrolled down the list looking and examining each picture.

When she reached through the entire list, she saw that none of them were Brandon. Kami's eyes started to tear up with disappointment as she turned around and sat in the chair behind her. Her hopes were crushed, smashed. She put her head into her hands and unleashed all of her tears. Johnny jumped up off the table and walked over to Kami, placing his arm across her shoulders; he held on to her while Zak went over to the computer and started to do something on it.

After a few minutes, Jon led Kami out of the room and into the living room to get a drink and calm down. Zak, on the other hand, didn't leave; instead he stayed typing away.

Later that night, at around eleven, Zak finally came out of the computer room and went straight to Kami's room. He knocked on the door, and Kami yelled, "Come in!" Her voice softly carried through the door. Zak opened it and treaded in. Kami's eyes were a soft red as if she had been crying for hours and rubbing the tears from her eyes. She was in a pair of pink pajamas that Rachel had loaned her.

A soft and sensitive feeling swept over Zak as he saw her. When Zak shut the door behind him, Kami looked at him and thanked him, "Thank you so much for trying, and sorry for breaking down. It's just that I've known him for so long, and, well…he's my friend, my best friend, and it's just so hard not knowing where he is or if he's in trouble or even if he's alive."

Zak looked up and replied, "It's all right. I just wanted you to know that we are going to find him. I promise."

Kami ran up to him and gave him a friendly hug and said softly, "Thank you. Thank you so much for everything." Zak just gave a small smile and put his arms around her.

⸙–⸙

The next morning as Kami slept in, Zak was talking to the others in the living room about leaving to go out and find Brandon. "Hey, do you guys mind if we go out and search for Brandon?" asked Zak.

"No, but how are we going to get around?" questioned Katherine.

"Well my parents own a mountain truck, and they said that it was all right if I take it to help her, and we have our weapons if the Seekers attack," answered Zak to Katherine.

Jon and Rachel looked at each other as Rachel stood

up to get a cup of coffee and gave her opinion. "I have no problem with it. What do you guys say?"

Jon replied, "Road trip!" And Katherine nodded her head.

"I have no complaints, and it gives us something to do instead of lying around here like a bunch of couch potatoes!"

※—※

When Kami woke up, she drifted into the living room still half-asleep. She didn't see anyone on the white sofa or in the white arm chair and not even leaning on the shady blue walls. She went into the kitchen, and still no one was there, only a half pot of coffee on the marble counters. Kami went into all the rooms looking for someone, but no one showed.

Kami sat on the couch and waited for someone to pop up.

Finally Katherine came out from in the kitchen and saw Kami lying on the couch. "Hey, you awake?" Kami jumped and sat up, turning around.

"Yea. Where were you guys?"

Katherine's eyes popped, and she exclaimed, "Oh sorry, we never showed you the basement, the other basement. But first go get changed out of Rachel's pj's and into one of my outfits, okay!" Kami nodded her head and went into her room.

When Kami came out fully awake, she had on a knee-length light green jean skirt, a pink tank top, and a white jacket. Katherine stayed out in the living room waiting. "Okay, now that you're ready, follow me."

Kami replied with uncertainty, "Okay."

Katherine took her through the kitchen, through the pantry, and through and door that was in the pantry. That's when she revealed the huge basement.

Parked in the basement was a double-door grayish mountain truck, and all around it were Rachel, Jon, and Zak. Kami's jaw dropped in amazement as Katherine kept walking, pulling Kami along with her by her arm. Zak looked up and so did the others as Jon and Rachel shouted with happiness, "Surprise! We're going to go out and help you find Brandon!"

Kami started to tear up with joy as she shouted back at everyone, "Oh my gosh! Are you serious! Thank you so much! You guys don't have to do this."

Jon spoke up and announced, "Yes, we do, *but* Zak is the one who first brought it up, and this truck is his!" Kami looked over at Zak and smiled as she continued down the stairs.

Once she hit the solid floor, Kami trotted over to him and cheerfully thanked him. "Thank you, but how did you get this?"

"I come from a rich family."

Kami continued to smile and turned to look at the truck. "Wow, this thing is huge!"

Rachel walked over to Kami. "Well, we're leavin' today, and we are already packed, so if you want to go, hurry up and pack!" Kami took off for the stairs, skipping steps on the way up, and flew out of the door, but then came back gliding her head in through the doorway. "Wait, why do I have to pack? I don't have clothes or anything!" exclaimed Kami, Rachel looked at Katherine, and they both yelled back.

"Sure you do. Go look in the box under the table in the computer room!" Kami nodded happily and took off for the room.

The minute Kami reached the computer room she looked under the table and grabbed the box. She pulled it out and opened it; in it were brand-new clothes of many bright colors and new patterns. This was something she hadn't seen in a long time, since she'd been in the same ones ever since the age of ten. There were so many. She turned around, about to leave, but as she started to, she heard a profound breathing coming from behind, and blanket of uneasiness enveloped her. She turned around to check and see if it was just her imagination, but when she did, she saw a silhouetted figure staring at her. At first it seemed as though the figure was a Seeker, but the tension in the room didn't feel as if it was. The figure stepped forward into the light, wearing a tight black shirt, black skinny jeans, and shoes. The moment Kami saw what the figure was, her jaw fell to the floor with the box following.

Her eyes glittered with disbelief, because standing in front of her was Brandon. Certain things about him were the same, the face, and the look. As for other things like his clothes and eyes, they were different—especially the eyes. They were different because they had a certain glow to them that she couldn't make out. It seemed as if he had no soul. But Kami didn't care, because standing in front of her was her lifelong friend. Brandon didn't say anything but just stood there staring at her, as if he was waiting for something. Kami hesitated to walk forward and asked, "Brandon...is that...really you?"

4

"No! Please, stop! Stop! Don't do this to her!" cried out Brandon as he jolted forward against the chains that held him back with all of his might.

"Too late, Brandon. She's going to think it's you, and when she goes with the Seeker, it will kill her and destroy her lifeless body!" yelled the mad man.

"No! Why are you doing this?" yelled Brandon as he gave up, breathing intensely.

"Because, Brandon! Because! You can thank your father for all of this; it's all because of him!"

"What could he have done that was so horrible that I don't know about? Nothing, because he told his family everything."

"Did you know that he was a murderer?" questioned the mad man loudly.

"My dad was no murderer!" shouted back Brandon in denial as he tried to move. The mad man smirked.

"Oh yes he was. He killed my brother when he tested this 'cure' that your father *knew* was unstable, and now look! My brother is dead!"

"Then why are you taking your hate out on me? My

father is dead too! And it's because of *your* creatures! So you've already had your revenge."

"Well, I didn't get the joy of watching him die!" the guy replied sickly as he gave a snotty look and continued, he stepped right up in Brandon's face, spitting as he spoke. "So I'll take the next best thing—his son!"

Brandon revealed a disgusted look and spit in the mad man's face; he backed up, wiping the spit off as Brandon asked, "Who are you anyway?"

"You're in no position to be doing such things when you're chained to a wall by your arms and being forced to watch your 'beloved girlfriend' die in front of you! Oh, and you want to know the best part?" Brandon made no comment, which angered the mad man, making him slap Brandon across the face. "Answer me when I ask you a question!"

Brandon looked at him and answered with hate and dislike in his tone. "What?" Then dropped his head to his chest.

"You know what; I just hatched a brilliant idea! I was going to 'test' this on your father, but I've decided to test it on you! You're lucky that I made some major adjustments to it though!" He grinned evilly. "So, do you know what I'm going to *make* you do?"

Brandon looked up and answered with a cocky attitude, "You can't make me do anything!"

The mad man smirked again. "I'm going to force you to *kill* your girlfriend!"

"You can't make me do that! I wouldn't do anything for you, but especially not *that!*"

"Of course I can. I can make you do anything I want you to." The mad man walked in front of Brandon, pulling something out of his lab coat. Seeing what the mad man pulled out, Brandon struggled to get free.

"What! What are you—." As Brandon tried to finish that last sentence, two Seekers came up and punched him across the face, left side to right over and over until he bled from both cheeks. A mix of saliva and blood dripped from Brandon's mouth as he fell forward, unable to hit the ground, as he was hanging by his arms. They then hit him in the gut till he was forced to gasp for air, breathing deeply and heavily, taking in each punch, then they clawed his arms and face, watching blood rush out.

All Brandon could do was hang there taking in the blows till he was near losing consciousness. The punches caused him to have a black eye, but he could still see a blurred-up dark green thing coming at him. Before he could feel anything else, he lost all consciousness while the Seekers held him up against the wall.

❧❧

Just as Kami started to believe that the person in front of her was Brandon, Jon came running in. "Hey, sorry to—." Jon looked into the eyes of "Brandon" and yelled at Kami, "Stop! Do not walk forward!"

Kami turned around and asked, "Why? This is Brandon."

Jon ran up to her and yanked her away, as the "Brandon" just stood there. "That's *not* Brandon." Kami looked at him.

"How do you know?"

"Because, look into its eyes and tell me what you see. Are they like Brandon's?" Kami did what she was told and stared into the eyes of the puppet in front of her, all she saw was a dark glow, when suddenly they burst into a glowing red ball. Kami turned away, due to the bright light from the thing. She looked at "Brandon" but didn't see him; instead she saw a Seeker. It then sprint-limped forward at Jon. There was nothing he could use to defend himself, he tried to punch it, but the Seeker's body was like a wall. The Seeker grabbed Jon and held him by the neck, choking him.

Kami reached into her bag and pulled out her whip. She pressed the button and the chain flew out as she started to swing it around to her side. She walked closer and closer, sweat was running down her cheeks. She was so scared that either she was going to hit Jon, or if by a small chance she killed it, the Seeker would kill Jon before death.

As she aimed and forced the whip at the Seeker, a jolt of guilt hit her in her gut. *What if it kills him? What if I kill him?* Kami shut her eyes and tightened them.

When she opened her eyes, she saw Jon lying on the floor. She couldn't see if he was breathing or not, so she bent down to check if he had a pulse, but felt nothing. Kami's eyes started to tear up as she turned around to yell for help, but when she turned back to look at Jon, he was right in her face, eyes wide open and lips tucked in as if he was about to burst out laughing. Kami jumped back, about to have a heart attack and stood up as Jon laughed his guts out. He laughed so hard that tears came down from his eyes. Kami asked while breathing heavily, "How did you do that? I checked your pulse."

After Jon wiped the tears from his eyes, he answered, "You pressed in the wrong spot! Last time I checked, your pulse could be checked on the neck, not the forehead. Oh and by the way, that's the way to check for a fever!"

Kami looked at him and blushed, kicking him lightly on the side. "Be quiet! I'm sorry that I didn't know!" Johnny continued to laugh. She grabbed the box and started to walk out, but then stopped and turned around. "So *did* I hit the Seeker?" Jon looked up and answered still laughing a little. "Yea. Nice job by the way!" He winked. Kami smiled and walked out of the room.

As soon as Kami finished packing and put everything in piles, she walked into the living room where everyone else lounged around. She sat down on the couch and stared at everyone while they talked over the plan. "Okay, since the country is divided into four territories, and the main cities are on each on the corners of the territories and we're in the center, we will go to Brownten first since it's on the top, then southwest to Broad City, after that down to Lenowa, and lastly to Wenstal," announced Zak.

Katherine stood up and asked, "So what happens if he's not in any of those cities?"

Everyone formed an odd silence for a minute until Rachel answered the question. "Then we head to the coast of Wenstal and check the islands such as Stravage Island, Carina, and Banner Village." No one objected, so that seemed to be the plan.

Jon then stood, asking a very important question, "So what if we come across Seekers? I mean, what about Kami? She doesn't really have *any* experience."

Zak thought about it for a sec then answered, "Okay, Kami, listen up, and you guys need to too. When you're fighting a Seeker or a pack, you always want to strike them below the head because their hands are *always* guarding their heads, and as we all know, their bladelike nails grow at will, so they can either, one, kill you or, two, severely injure you.

"Another thing is that they can shape shift. I don't know if all of them can, but I do know that some can. In order to tell if someone is real, look into their eyes, and you'll see something either normal or odd, as if it doesn't have a soul. And I tell you this because the 'eyes are the key to the soul.' If they're different, then get away, or if they know you know that they're fake, they'll attack, so fight back and call for help. Now if there is something like a vase, throw something else at it, and if it's a Seeker, it will come out of its stage and will either attack or run.

"As for Kami, someone will need to be with her at *all* times, since we don't know what they're after, which may be her or could have been Brandon the other times. She'll need to be guarded."

When everyone was ready to leave, Kami jumped in the truck and sat there quiet as a mouse. No one asked what was wrong or anything since they figured that they knew what was wrong.

Kami had just seen what she thought was Brandon, and to tell you the truth, everyone knew that she liked him more than a friend, and from the way it sounded, he liked her the same way back.

Once everyone buckled in, Zak started the truck to begin the journey of a lifetime.

5

After about seven days of driving with a few stops at motels, Zak finally announced that they were almost to the first city. The whole time Kami had looked out the window hoping that she maybe, just maybe, she would happen to see Brandon somewhere on the road. The instant they pulled into the parking lot in front of the city hall of Brownten, Kami's hopes and dreams were shattered.

The city looked like a dump; dead trees were along the roads; no one was outside except for the punks of the place; there was no color to it; the houses looked old and ratty; street lamps had broken bulbs; glass, trash, and other kinds of litter crowded the streets; and the grass of the town was burned and almost completely turned into dirt.

They all climbed out of the truck and into the lot. Zak looked at them and explained some things, "Okay, we're here, and we're going in to talk to the mayor; I don't want any of you guys opening your big mouths." He paused, staring at Jon, so did everyone else, and Jon smiled then put his hand over his mouth. Zak then went on. "Unless asked a question. The mayor of Brownten is *very* touchy, and if you say one odd thing, he'll get very suspicious of you. Okay? And trust me, we don't want that." He turned to Kami, who was leaning up against the truck looking at the other part of the city. "Are you going to be okay with going in there, or do you want to stay out here?"

Kami looked at him and replied very softly, "Yea, I'll be fine."

The moment they reached the front of the mayor's office, the gang could here a loud discussion going on inside until an angered man flung the door open, storming out of the office, leaving the door open behind him. Zak popped his head in, seeing no one in there, he tapped on the door. "Knock, knock." And he walked in signaling the others to follow. The mayor glanced up from behind his computer and reached over his desk to shake Zak's hand.

"Well, well, look who it is. Zak Delltoria, how have you been?"

"Just fine, and you?"

Kami turned to Katherine and whispered, "How do they know each other?"

Katherine looked to the corner of her eye, still facing the two, and replied, "Well, since Zak comes from a rich family, he has a lot of connections to people in power. His parents are like best friends with the mayors of each city." Kami awed a silent awe and continued to listen.

"So, Zak, what are you up to?"

Zak shrugged. "Well, I came here to ask a favor."

The mayor looked to the side to try and see behind Zak. "Who are your friends?"

Zak looked behind him and stepped back toward

Jon. "This is Jon." He pointed to Katherine. "That is Katherine, and the one beside her is Rachel." Zak scooted Jon over to the other side and put his arm over Kami's shoulder. "And this is Kami. She needs your help to find her friend by the name of Brandon."

The mayor looked at her, "Okay, how can I help?" Zak stepped forward.

"Well, she was taken from her home and put in this forest by the Seekers, and about month ago, we found her in the middle of the sidewalk. She says that the Seekers attacked her again, and this time her friend didn't make it through the blur that the Seekers created. So have you seen a guy with brown eyes, brown hair, a natural build, and a tough-guy face, oh and he's eighteen?"

The mayor looked at his computer screen and started to type. Zak looked at Katherine, Rachel, and Kami. "Hey, this is going to take a while. Do ya'll want to look around the city?"

Rachel nodded her head and replied, "Yea, that sounds good." Katherine and Kami nodded and headed for the door.

As the three walked around the city, they began to talk about how Katherine, Rachel, Jon, and Zak knew each other. "So you guys have been friends for quite some time then." confirmed Kami.

"Yea," answered Katherine.

"So how did you guys become friends?" wondered Kami.

"Well when we were in high school, all the guys were the flirt type. Katherine and I were juniors at the time when Jon and Zak came up to us and started to hit on us, but after we talked for a while, they kinda backed off, and we just became friends," answered Rachel.

Kami looked confused, "What are juniors? And high school?"

Katherine looked a Kami and tried to explain in the easiest way. "High school is the last part of school, unless you want to go to another school called college, and juniors are the second to last grade till you're done."

"Oh okay, that makes sense. Were Jon and Zak juniors?"

"No, they were the last grade of high school, called seniors," corrected Rachel.

Then Katherine bumped in. "At that time I was sixteen, along with Rachel. Jon was seventeen, and Zak was eighteen. But now I'm twenty-one, so is Rachel. Jon is twenty-two, and Zak is twenty-three."

"Wow, I feel so young compared to you guys 'cause I'm just eighteen," exclaimed Kami while the other two laughed.

It had been an hour and thirty minutes since they started walking around, and it was about three o'clock when they stopped at a little place to rest and get something to drink. The walls of the place had chipped paint of different vibrant colors; the tables were funky shaped, sort of a mix between a triangle and a square and decorated with these bead-looking things that were shiny. Everyone in there looked preppy and happy as if they were just purposed to by the man of their dreams, or they just proposed to the woman and she said yes.

A girl who looked about eighteen walked up to them and asked, "Is there anything I can get you? A Dipremo, Serep?"

Kami looked way confused, so Rachel leaned over and whispered, "Those are drinks by the way." But

Katherine looked up at the girl, "No thanks. Just three waters, please."

The girl nodded her head. "Okay I'll get that for you. If you need anything, just holler. My name is Cary by the way." And she skipped over to the bar not far from the table.

"So what was Brandon like?" Katherine and Rachel both asked. Kami held the tooth from her necklace in her fingers.

"Well, he was so nice, sweet, funny, loving, caring, and so cute," answered Kami,

Katherine lowered her head and laid it on her fist listening to every little detail about Brandon. "Wow, he does sound like the perfect guy." Just as Katherine finished her sentence, Rachel's cell phone rang.

Kami jumped into the air, looking for the noise, asking in a startled tone "what was that?" as Rachel pulled it out.

"Hello. Uh yea, one sec." She stood up and walked outside of the building.

Just then Cary walked back over with a tray full of waters. "Okay, here are your three waters. Can I get you anything else?" she said as she slowly placed each water perfectly on a coaster.

Katherine shook her head. "No, but thank you." Cary smiled and nodded her head then walked off.

Katherine leaned over and tried to explain what a cell phone was. "A cell phone is a thing that you can use to contact others, almost anywhere you want to. By calling and texting. What Rachel is doing is a call, okay?"

Kami nodded her head and asked, "So who do you think she's talking to?" Kami took a sip of her water as Katherine finished taking hers.

"My guess is Zak, but it could be Jon. You never can tell because they always switch with who calls, and their voices sound the same on the phone too." Kami giggled as Rachel walked back in, sat down, and took a drink of her water.

"That was Zak. He and the mayor just finished the city search." Rachel's voice softened as she continued. "The results... they didn't find him, but we still have like three cities to go and another three villages, so our hopes aren't crushed. We'll find him," she assured. "But now Zak wants us to head back to city hall."

Everyone took one last drink of water then stood up. Rachel laid three dollars on the table and followed the others out the door.

Just as the three were about to city hall, the sidewalk in front of them started to blur; the girls jumped back. Katherine and Rachel reached for their weapons and stood ready to fight. Kami stood there hoping that the thing coming out of the blur would, this time, be Brandon, and without thinking, didn't grab her whip.

The thing coming out of the blur, was rising up from the ground, slow and steady. In front of them stood something that looked like a black bulge slouching over. There was nothing to it, no eyes, mouth, nose, or even a figure. All it did was... stand there. Katherine and Rachel lowered their weapons and started to study the object in front of them. When suddenly the bulge swung around and sprang at them, swinging its long blade, swiftly and quietly.

Caught off guard and unable to use their weapons, the bulge knocked the two girls into the air and sliced down their arms as they fell to the ground. Breathless and in pain, they just lay there as if they had died. The being went for Kami, sprinting toward her, looking as if it were gliding across the floor. As soon as it reached two feet from her, it stopped. Now she could see something glittering from underneath the black robe. It looked like eyes, but only one, and the rest of it was hidden from the shadow of the robe. It just stood there with one arm open and the other with the blade in it.

Kami started to back up slowly, struck with fear. She was trembling, her eyes full of pure terror, her lips quaking with the insecurity of what would happen next. She tucked in her lips and licked them over and over nervously. *Run or fight or wait to see what happens?* Those were the choices running circles through her mind. Kami soon went back too far; she hit a tall brick wall, and about ten feet straight in front of her still just standing there, was the bulge.

After a minute or so, the bulge started to slowly walk forward, step by step, but as it did, it lifted up its arm toward what looked to be a hood and slowly unveiled itself.

6

Kami's heart pounded and pounded as the black hand reached to the hood of the robe. Slowly pulling the hood off little by little to reveal, standing in front of her was Brandon, again. His face looked scarred up as if he had been beaten, his right eye was a little blacker than the other, and he had little cuts still all over his face. Kami didn't seem too surprised but instead stared into the eyes of the being in front of her. She couldn't see anything but emptiness, nothing. Until she heard a small and quiet voice whisper to her, "Come with me, Kami. It's me, Brandon. Come with me, and we won't have to deal with these people or Seekers ever again. We can go back to the forest or even our village and have things the way they used to be." Brandon stuck out his hand signaling her to come with him.

Kami's eyes sparkled as she thought about how nice the option would be; memories of her childhood suddenly came rushing back to her.

"Tag, you're it!" yelled out Brandon as he started running.

"I'm gonna get you!" shouted back Kami, and she started to run after him.

"Ha ha you can't catch me, 'cause you're too slow!" bragged Brandon as he ran behind a house.

"I'm gonna make you eat those words!" replied Kami as she sped up. The two ran around playing and calling each other names for a couple of hours and finally stopped to get a snack from Brandon's house. They sat on the porch eating their granola bars and talked.

"So what do you want to do tomorrow?" asked Kami.

"I don't know, maybe go down to the river and get a boat," suggested Brandon.

Kami smiled and replied, "Yea, that sounds fun. We should do that." Brandon nodded his head.

"Then I guess that's what we're going to do!" he smiled.

Kami suddenly jumped out of her daze and yelled, "No, no, you're not Brandon!" She stepped back to pull her whip out of her bag. Having her heart filled to the brim with hate for the monster in front of her, she switched open the whip. "Why are you trying to hurt me?! Why do you take the shape of Brandon just to hurt me?" Kami yelled. She twirled the whip around above her head and swung it at Brandon. Brandon, at the last second, jumped back and drew his blade, blocking the whip. Kami pulled the chain back and swung it in a circle to her side as she walked forward. Brandon just stood there waiting for her next move. Kami unleashed the chain at Brandon with all of her might, but Brandon blocked it again. Kami yanked the whip back, spinning around. She threw the end of the whip at his face, but he parried the attempt. Kami leaned on her back leg, regaining balance; once she was set, she sprinted at Brandon. She flung the whip in every direction at the phony with fury. With every swing though, Brandon connected it with his blade. Kami, trying desperately to finish him off, leaped in the air, holding the whip high above, but this time the chain wrapped around his blade. Brandon pulled back his blade, taking Kami's weapon from her and throwing it behind him.

Weaponless Kami turned around and started to run; she ran, turning corners and dodged any and all objects that tried to stop her. Tears ran down her cheeks as she remembered Rachel and Katherine lying back there defenseless. Kami turned around checking on her progress on ditching Brandon, and to her surprise he wasn't anywhere in sight. She stopped and looked around, making sure the coast was clear. Slouching down to catch her breath, Kami thought of why the thing in front of her could talk. *Seekers can't talk, at least that's what I thought, and if that was Brandon why would he attack me... No, no it wasn't him,* thought Kami as she regained her breath. She looked around and noticed that she was in an alley, with clothes hanging from lines above her. Dark brick walls surrounded her, except for the opening that she came in through. It was a dead end.

Kami started to walk toward the opening with caution, when suddenly something grabbed her arms and gripped around her the neck, holding its hand over her mouth. Kami tried to scream, but it started to squeeze her mouth tighter. The being clenched her arms, and shoved what felt like bracelets, onto her wrists. Her wrists felt like they were burning, about to fall off when a familiar voice started to speak, "You can run, but you can't hide." Kami knew that the voice belonged to the phony Brandon. She squealed and started to jump and kick around frantically as she tried to take in what little air she could. She shook her head and tried to get loose, but nothing would work; he had a very tight grip on her and wouldn't let go.

Suddenly the hand holding her mouth let go, but only to grab something else, she now felt something sharp and cold touching the skin on her neck. "I gave you a chance to live, but you didn't want it, so I guess this is the only way." He lifted up his blade. Kami shut her eyes tightly and started to pray, when she barely heard another familiar voice speak from a distance.

"Let her go!" shouted Zak with a determined tone as he jumped from the top of an alley building.

Brandon removed the bracelets before he forced Kami to the ground, knocking her unconscious. He turned to look at Zak. "Well, look who we have here. The famous Zak Delltoria here to save the day and his sidekick Jon Tenoria. This ought to be fun." Brandon expressed sarcastically as he stood ready to fight with a grin on his face, his legs were separated with his left hand hanging down and his right holding the blade in the air waiting for Zak and Johnny to make the first move.

"Who are you?" asked Zak as he stepped into his stance, his feet were planted apart, his left hand was holding the black blade while the right was ready to grab on at any given moment.

Before Brandon could answer, Jon added on, "By the way, I'm not his sidekick!" As he stood in his stance, his feet were apart and his arms separated against his chest with the creshens in place.

Still in his stance, Brandon answered, "Simple answer, but why should I tell you?"

Zak was losing patience and yelled out, "Why do you want her?!"

"Well, my name is... On second thought, I'll have *her* tell you." Brandon pointed at Kami, who lay unconscious on the ground. Brandon lunged forward toward Zak; Zak blocked the attack with his blade. Jon rolled to the side and went to attack Brandon from behind, but Brandon countered it with a second blade. Holding the two back, Brandon laughed. "Is this all you guys have!" He shoved Zak's and Jon's weapons at them and backed up. Brandon stood in front of them holding one blade out and the other up high, waiting to see what would happen next. Zak and Jon sprang at Brandon with fury, swinging their weapons over and over with every block Brandon made.

The battle lasted a while before Katherine and Rachel came running in, not wanting to be a disturbance to the battle, they went over to Kami. Zak shoved Brandon to the floor and held him at blade point. "Now *you* will tell me who you are!"

Brandon grinned. "You fight quite well, and so do you, Jon." Jon smirked and jogged over toward Kami.

Zak was getting more upset by the second and started to yell even louder, "Answer the question! Who are you?"

Brandon frowned and replied, "You don't have to yell."

Zak restrained himself from beating Brandon to a pulp and asked the same question.

"So you care more about the little pain she's in instead of the huge amount that I'm in. Whatever, just think about who I look like." The ground underneath Brandon turned to a blur, as Brandon was being sucked in; he saluted Zak in a cocky way and whispered. "I look forward to our next meeting." Zak jumped back, putting away his blade, and walked over toward Kami who was waking up.

The instant Zak knelt down beside her, Kami tried to ask him something. "Did, did you kill him?"

Zak answered concerned, "No, he slipped away. Why? Do you know him?" With the help of Jon and Rachel, Kami stood up. "Yes, that was Brandon." Everyone's jaws dropped, and Katherine looked at Kami.

"Are you sure? Maybe you hit your head a little too hard or something and just saw things."

"Yes, I'm sure, that is what he looks like on the outside, but...on the inside that wasn't him. He would never act like that." Everyone looked relieved, and Kami continued, "The first time I saw him, when he hurt Katherine and Rachel; he stopped in front of me. I looked into his eyes; there was nothing, like an empty shell. And as you all know, he could speak, which ruled out the idea that he was a Seeker, I think. Nevertheless, what I don't know is what was that thing that in front of us, if it wasn't a Seeker?"

"Well, you have one thing right: Seekers can't talk and there are not many things that can look just like someone like that. That might have been Brandon...just something could be controlling him. I don't know what or how," suspected Zak.

Kami stood in front of Katherine and Rachel. "Sorry for what he did to you and for not fighting. I just hoped that *was* Brandon, the real one."

Katherine and Rachel nodded and replied, "It's okay."

Kami then turned to Zak and Jon. "Thanks for coming, but how did you know that we were in trouble, and where to find me?"

Jon spoke up and answered the questions. "Well, I received a text, like a call but spelled out, that said that you were in trouble, so we came. When we arrived, you were running away and Brandon was behind you, so we just followed." Kami smiled and thanked them as they walked back to truck to head out for Broad City.

7

Why, why did I do that? What's happening to me? thought Brandon as he sat in his cell with his hands chained above his head to the wall, when he heard a hateful voice over the intercom, "I told you I could make you do whatever I wanted you to do. And I must say that the way you spoke was just perfect; the sarcasm fit right in." Brandon looked around but didn't say anything. He just sat there, until a door opened and in came the mad man with two large Seekers.

"Why were those words being spoken when I wasn't the one saying them? And how did I…fight like that?" asked Brandon quietly.

"Well, actually you are the one saying them; I just tell you what to say. The information travels straight into your brain, making you say them, and you have no choice or control; all you can do is watch. This is the same with fighting; I look up the best techniques and pretty much download them into your brain."

"Then how is it going in my brain?"

"It's all because of the…" The mad man stopped speaking, catching himself before he gave too much information. "I don't want to spoil the surprise!" He then started to pace around the room. "But you did like the two blades I gave you, didn't you?"

Brandon slowly and sickly nodded his head and asked, "How are you doing this?" The mad man stopped and walked toward Brandon; he bent down and lifted up his chin to make Brandon look him in the eyes.

"That's something you don't need to know."

He popped Brandon's chin in the air, making it hit his chest once it fell back down. The mad man stood up and signaled the Seekers to do something as he walked out of the room. The Seekers stepped closer to Brandon; they punched him across the face a couple times then in the gut a few more times, forcing Brandon to struggle for air, then unlocked his arms from the chain and walked out of the room. Brandon fell face first to the brick floor, while his bloody spit went everywhere.

Carrying himself with what little strength he had, over to a corner, tears started down Brandon's face as he sat up and prayed, "Oh God, please help Kami. Keep her safe along with Zak, Jon, Rachel, and Katherine. Please help this mad man learn that you're there for him. And please help me, amen." Brandon's eyelids felt like weights. He yawned in agony and cuddled into a ball to fall slowly asleep in misery on the cold, hard floor of his cellar.

※ ※

After six days and five nights, they reached Broad City. And this time on the trip, Kami wasn't just staring out the window; she was full of excitement and happiness.

As they passed through the gate, a gorgeous city

opened up in front of them. Kids were playing outside with their toys or riding their bikes; bright flowers were planted everywhere; long tall trees grew healthy; a variety of beautiful houses were lined up perfectly in long rows; sparkling water flowed from one part of the river to the next; and everything seemed to be so peaceful. They pulled into the parking lot and reeled out of the truck. The air smelled wonderful. Kami had a feeling that maybe, just maybe, the real Brandon was here.

As they stepped out of the truck and into the open, a wonderful smell overwhelmed them, making them all feel happy and upbeat. "So how is this mayor; is he like the last one?" asked Johnny.

"No, and this one is a woman. She is very laid back and has her advisors take care of everything," answered Zak. "But still watch what you say and only speak when spoken to."

The group walked up the stairs and into the city hall. They crossed a few halls and went around a couple corners until they finally came across the door of the mayor's office. Before they knocked on the door, Zak gave them one last talk, but Kami sort of ignored it and looked around. She suddenly heard her name being whispered, "Kami, Kami."

Kami looked up swiftly; she saw no one, then turned to Jon and asked, "Did you say my name?" Jon shook his head, and Kami turned to Zak. "Sorry to interrupt, but did you say my name?"

Zak looked at her. "No, I didn't."

Kami looked at Rachel and Katherine. "Did you guys?" They both shook their heads, and Kami looked puzzled. "Then who did?" Everyone just stared at Kami with confusion.

"Dude, no one said your name. You're just hearing things."

When the mayor's office opened up, the five walked in with Zak leading. The woman in the office sat in a medium-sized black leather chair. She turned her head from the computer screen.

"Zak, darling, how have you been? Looks like you've been doing great since the last time I saw you!" She tottered off her chair and walked around her desk to give Zak a big hug.

Zak seemed embarrassed as he answered back, "Nice, nice, and you?" The mayor released her grip on Zak and looked at him as he finished what he was saying, "Things working out nice? The city looks wonderful!" She looked at Zak and smiled.

"Why thank you. The citizens of Broad City have worked very hard on sculpting the city to where it is now." She paused and looked behind Zak. "So what brings you here, and who are your friends?"

Zak turned around and stepped back, then pointed to the person as he said each name, "Well, that is Jon." Jon smiled as Zak continued. "Rachel, Katherine." They both copied Jon and smiled pleasantly. "And this is Kami. She is the reason why we are here. She needs your help." The mayor stepped forward and shook Kami's hand then smiled a sort of fake-looking smile, as if she had something to hide.

"So what do you need?" Zak stepped back to his original spot and answered the question.

"Well, we need your help tracking down a person

that was lost. His name is Brandon, he's eighteen and has brown eyes, a natural build, straight brown hair, and tough-guy face. By chance have you seen him around?"

The mayor looked puzzled for a moment then the light bulb lit. "Oh yea, a guy came by fitting those descriptions just like two hours ago. I don't know if he's still here, but it wouldn't hurt to look around."

Zak then asked, "Couldn't we just search him on the master computer?"

The mayor looked down and replied in a soft tone. "No, I'm sorry to say this, but two Seekers came by a few moments after Brandon came and destroyed it." She looked up. "Our best men are working on it right now. I'm so sorry."

"Wait, what did Brandon want?" asked Kami. The mayor's smile turned into a look of worry as if she just remembered something very terrible.

"Well," replied the mayor, as she swallowed a nervous gulp of saliva, "he came by and said that...um, well...that if a girl by the name of Kami and with your description came by, he would know and he would come after you, and anyone who stepped in his way would be killed even if it was one of my people."

As the last few words escaped the mayor's mouth, all eyes glued to Kami. Her eyes started to water as she looked around the room, slowly replying, "Okay, thank you." Kami put her hand over her mouth and a tear ran down her cheek, then she dropped her hand to speak. "I'll be sure to leave as soon as possible...Now if you'll please excuse me, I'll be just outside the room." Kami turned toward the door and walked out closing it behind her.

After the door shut completely, Zak turned to Katherine and Rachel and asked them, "Will you two go out there with her just in case he does show up?" The two girls nodded and walked out of the room.

The two turned to see Kami praying. They stayed quiet and walked a few feet away to give Kami her privacy.

"Dear heavenly Father, I pray that you would please help us find Brandon. Lord, I also pray that we can get him back to normal…" A few tears fell to the floor as she continued. "And Lord, thank you so much for allowing me to find Zak, Jon, Katherine, and Rachel; they have been just so wonderful. I want to thank you for all the help that I've received from everyone. Thank you, amen." Kami gazed up for a second then glanced to the side to see Katherine and Rachel sitting on a bench on the other side of the door, whispering to each other, not wanting to bother Kami. Kami rose and asked, "Hey, can I ask you guys a sort of personal question?" The two nodded, and Kami went ahead. "Do you guys know what being 'saved' is?"

Katherine looked at Rachel and replied, "No, why? What is it?" Kami smiled.

"It is God's gift to man. Sin isn't allowed in heaven, and since we're all sinners, we shouldn't be allowed in, and the penalty for sin is death, so we should die and burn in hell. But God sent his only son, Jesus, down from heaven to live a sinless life and be crucified on the cross to pay the penalty of death so that all our sin would be washed away so that we could live in heaven. Though he died, Jesus rose again and went back to heaven. And if we ask God, aloud, for the gift of salvation and admit that we are sinners, have faith that Jesus died on the cross and rose again, and have faith in him, we will be saved. That way, once you die, you will not burn in hell, but instead you will go to heaven with God."

Katherine and Rachel had a look of remembrance. "Yea, we knew about that. Our parents told us when we were little."

Kami glowed with joy. "Good, with all this happening, I just wanted to see…"

Once they were all done in the hall, the three walked back into the mayor's office and saw her on an intercom speaking. "Attention, attention, Broad City inhabitants, please go straight to your homes and do not, I repeat *do not* come out. Working adults, head home and lock up your businesses up and keep your children indoors until further notice. Thank you. Announcement by Mayor Carissa Laviente." She took her hand off the button and turned toward the group.

Zak looked at the three. "Okay, Carissa has allowed us to use her city to stop Brandon, but the problem is that I don't know how we are going to do it."

Everyone pondered on the thought for a second when Kami stepped forward. "I have a plan." All eyes were on her. "We are going to lure Brandon into a secluded area and take him there. Someone or something he wants will need to stand alone, and everyone else has to be hidden, ready to take him out at any given moment." The plan sounded all right, but one thing needed to be clarified.

Jon spoke up and asked nervously, "Sounds good, but… what are we going to use to lure him?"

Jon knew the answer but hoped that he was wrong; as Kami opened her mouth, the words came out low and quaky. "The one thing he wants—me."

8

"What are you thinking? You! No, no you're crazy! He will kill you!" screamed Zak with rage. "This is the only thing that we can do! I'm not going to put innocent lives at risk because of my problem! Not to mention that you guys will be waiting and watching for him to show up, and when he does, you'll jump down and knock him out!" Kami grew angrier by the second and just wanted Zak to understand. He sat in a chair in the far right corner of room, leaning it up against the wall on two legs with his arms crossed wearing a mask of anger.

Kami walked over and knelt down beside him as he dropped the chair on all fours. "Please, Zak, understand where I'm coming from. God will keep me safe, and who knows we might just be able to help him." Kami had calmed down and the tension in the room loosened. Jon put his hand on Zak's shoulder.

"Come on, Zak, she'll be fine. You and I will be up there."

Soon after, Katherine and Rachel walked up. "Please, Zak." Zak looked at them then back at Kami.

"You know what you need to do, right?" asked Jon.

"Yea, I'm going to walk into the intersection by myself, call out to him, and when he shows, you and Zak are going to jump down and knock him out."

Jon nodded and walked off then Katherine came up. "Aren't you nervous? Because you don't look like it. I am and I'm not even the one going in by myself."

"Yea, a little. But I'm kinda excited 'cause I might be able to help Brandon... Hey, you told Zak and Jon about what we had talked about the other day, right?"

"Yes, ma'am, and they believed me. It turns out that they already knew about it 'cause they went to the same church when they were little and the church taught salvation, so they were already saved."

"That's awesome, and it's also one of the reasons why I'm not nervous 'cause I know that if I were to die I would go to heaven so I really don't have a fear of dying."

"But I do have one question: how do *you* know about salvation?"

"Well, my village was a Christian Baptist village. It always had been, so everyone knew about it and went to the local church that also taught it. Both Brandon and I went to it, and sometimes, when we were younger, we would hide in the back, and we would take his sling shot with tiny items and sling them at the people in the pews, or we would hop up, once in a while, on our knees and tap a person on the head then duck under the pews, the person would search behind them and not see anything and start rubbing their head wondering what happened. It was so funny!"

Katherine started laughing with the picture in her mind as Rachel walked up. "What's up?"

"Nothing. You?" asked Kami.

"Nothing just helping with the setup…" Rachel responded. "Oh, by the way, Zak needs to talk to you."

Rachel, at that point, just walked away.

Kami walked over to Zak who sat working on a small device at a square table. "So whatcha doin'?" asked Kami in a playful tone.

"Just working on something that you will wear when you confront Brandon."

"What will it do?"

"It will allow me to hear everything that is said around you, so if you can hear something, I'll be able to hear it too, and I'll also be able hear everything that you say."

"So you'll be listening in on my private conversation with my—"Jon ran in, breathing hard, and interrupted Kami.

"Hurry, hurry! Brandon and a huge group of Seekers are coming this way!"

Everyone then rushed to finish the final jobs that had to be done and ran to their positions. Kami stood in the open with the small device in her ear waiting for him to show. She walked around and acted as if she never knew he was coming and mindlessly called out for him, holding onto the necklace that he made her.

Brandon came wearing his black robe with the hood down and the front open, he wore his tight black shirt and black skinny jeans, on each of his sides were the two blades, and as he walked toward her, the robe blew back gently with the breeze. He looked perfectly normal, no cuts or anything, unlike last time.

Brandon had blocked all the exits with Seekers and walked into the middle of the open intersection, a few feet away from Kami. "Well, well, look what I've found."

"Brandon, I know that isn't you speaking. It never has been; it's something else. I don't know what, but I know it's not you!"

"Silly girl, you know nothing. Oh, so you still have the necklace that I made you."

"No, *you* didn't make it; Brandon did!"

"You can think that, but *I* made it. In fact, I can tell you how."

Kami slightly looked over her shoulder and whispered, "Zak, it's time," but there was no answer. Kami tried talking again "Zak? Jon? Are you guys there?"

"If you're trying to contact your friends, don't!" Brandon then lifted up his finger and shook it at Kami. "Because I have them, you know Zak, Jon, Katherine, and Rachel."

A look of shock blew onto her face, then she tried to hide it. "What? What are talking about? I came here alone!"

Brandon rolled his eyes and looked at Kami with disappointment. "I'm very disappointed with you Kami. You know, it's not good to lie." He then lifted up his hand and snapped. In a matter of seconds, four Seekers came out of the crowd holding one of each of the gang by their arms, which were tied behind their backs. Kami's eyes grew huge, and her mouth dropped and hung open.

"How... how did you know?"

"Well, I would hate to spoil my magic trick by telling

you, so I guess maybe?" Brandon walked even closer there was now a two feet distance from them. "You know what, I might. I'll make a deal with you, and in the choices, I might offer to tell you. Choice one is that you come with me and I will let your friends go, and to throw in a bonus, I *may* tell you how I knew, but there are no guarantees. Choice two is that I kill your friends and tell you how I knew for sure and you still come with me. So which is it?"

Just as Kami opened her mouth to speak, something happened, something changed about Brandon, he fell to the ground holding his head and squirmed around, making sounds as if he were in tremendous pain. His muscles tightened, he started to sweat, his eyes opened and he spoke in a murderous screech, gulping the anguish down still holding in the cries.

"Kami, Kami..." He gave a tormented cry and continued, "You're right, right about every—." He yelled out, "Everything. It's not me; I would never do this to you!" He shouted in distress at this point; Kami ran to him, believing the Brandon in front of her was real.

She knelt down to try and comfort him, running her fingers through his hair gently, tears ran down her cheeks. He screamed out again. "I'm so sorry... sorry for everything I've done, but I have to tell you... that, that there is a mad man and..." He held his breath to hold in the pain then started to breathe harder. "Tell Zak, he would know... And, Kami, I love you. I love you so mu—"

Just then numerous deep cuts, massive bruises, and long scars, whip marks, claw marks, and burns appeared all over Brandon as he grabbed his head again and yelled with torture in his voice, then he suddenly stopped moving, yelling, and breathing. It seemed as if he just died but didn't.

Kami broke into tears as she stood up and backed away, fearing that the other Brandon, the horrible one, would come back. The lifeless body sunk into a blur that appeared under him, the Seekers followed their leader and disappeared into the blurs. The ones holding the captives let them go and followed the others.

Immediately after Zak, Jon, Katherine, and Rachel broke free from the bonds that held their arms together, they ran to Kami who stood a few feet away from where Brandon had disappeared, sobbing. "He...he's gone, where did he go?" she screamed desperately wanting answers, turning to Zak. "Is there any way for us to track him down? And who is this mad man that he was talking about?"

Zak's eyes grew, and worry overtook his voice as he backed away slowly. "Oh no...no, he can't be there. I knew that wasn't him saying those things. No, but I thought...How could he have escaped? Is he the reason for the Seekers coming back?"

"What, the Seekers 'coming back'? What is that supposed to mean? Have they been here before?" asked Jon.

Zak stopped moving. "Yes. Don't you remember?"

"Would I be asking if I remembered?" Jon was growing impatient and wanted answers. "Come on, Zak, tell us who this guy is! This is a clue to us finding and maybe saving Brandon's life!"

"Okay, okay, sit down."

9

"Kevin Beraldi is the name of the mad man, and he lived with his brother since he couldn't pay for his own house and both of his parents died in a car accident. The two had a very strong brotherly bond, and they looked out for each other. His brother's name was Jonathan Beraldi, and they both were scientists working on a cure for a common disease that killed many people.

"They both thought that they had created the cure and brought test subjects in who had the disease. They gave the 'cure' to the subjects, and that's when the unexplained things started to happen.

"The subjects' skin started to turn a sickly dark green color, and their eyes turned to a glowing bright red ball. The subjects' fingernails grew faster and sharper than the average human's. The curves developed on their toes and head. This was the beginning of the Seekers.

"Before the transformation took place, the signs of the disease went away, allowing the two to believe they found the cure. Knowing this, the two had given the vaccination to a big group of people." Zak stopped for a moment to take questions, but there were none so he continued. "When all the side effects worsened and people started to well... um, multiply on their own; the city folk started to worry. The 'cure' was discontinued, and the program was shut down. The test subjects were caged since they started to become violent, and a cure for them had begun.

"This is when a new guy was hired; his name was George Teonen. He had a small family one son and a wife—"

Just as Zak was about to go on, Kami interrupted him. "Oh my gosh! That must have been Brandon's dad!"

"Really? Why do you say that?" questioned Johnny.

"Because George Teonen was the name of Brandon's dad, but there's always a chance it could be someone else with the same name. Go ahead Zak."

"Well, George was pretty smart and ended up working with the two Beraldis. Together they came up with a possible cure that they tested on one of the now-known Seekers, but according to Kevin, George knew that it was unstable, but George claims that it was completely unknown on what the effects were. So they injected the possibility and hoped for the best. Jonathan was the one who volunteered to inject it, and the effects were that the Seeker's nails grew like knives and gave them the ability to shape shift.

"One day Jonathan and Kevin went in to check up on the subjects, but it turned out that one of the Seekers had squeezed loose and shape shifted into a desk chair. When Jonathan went to sit, the Seeker sprang at him right in front of Kevin and killed him. Ever since, Kevin held a grudge, blaming George for the making of the 'cure' since he came up with it.

"Sadly, without his brother, Kevin went insane; he started to try and murder George in his sleep. His attempt failed due to George's son who had wakened on the right night and caught Kevin in the act. George called the police, and they took him away.

"The Seekers, on the other hand, started going berserk; they banged on their cages and clawed at anyone who came by them. Until the lone Seeker who had escaped his prison came and released the rest. Now there where hundreds of Seekers with the ability to shape shift, but the reason why we don't know if all of them can is because not all of them were vaccinated, and those that were born as Seekers may not have inherited the ability. Get it?" Everyone nodded, and Zak continued, "Well, during the year that all this happened, the Seekers ended up freeing Kevin from his prison and took him as their leader for a reason we do not know, but he led them into the city and tried to kill George and continued to fail due to the team of police watching the house. George then feared for the safety of his family; in response to the fear, they moved to an unknown place in the middle of the night. Kevin grew angry and sent his Seekers across the world to find him.

"During this time, Kevin held his place in Andren and made sure that everything was under his control. He even invented many things that he showed to certain people, such as the rich, so I was able to see, but it was really nothing important.

"On July twenty-third, a secret police team snuck into the mansion where Kevin was living, using the cliff in the back, and they tried to kill him. When they busted through his door, Kevin called all the Seekers back to the mansion. Before the Seekers were able to transport there, the police had Kevin under custody and sent him to a mental hospital. The Seekers retreated back to the mansion and stayed there for the next two years waiting for their leader to come back.

"After two years passed, I guess the Seekers started to worry, so they attacked the hospital and grabbed Kevin. They headed back to the mansion and waited for Kevin to come back to himself.

"When he finally did, after about three months, Kevin sent the Seekers back around the world. Many people died last time, and now with the sudden attacks even more died. It was a very tragic day. The Seekers swept across the world, killing anything and everything that blocked their way. They must have found what they were looking for because the attacks everywhere else were dropping. However, the thing that we didn't understand was that after a while, like a week or two, Kevin's temper went off, and he sent Seekers to kill people in Andren."

Kami's eyes popped open, and she remembered Brandon's nightmares. "Oh my gosh, I know what happened there. Maybe Kevin wanted to watch George die, but instead the Seekers killed him. Brandon was telling me that when he was younger he could of sworn that something was in his window, which scared him, so he ran outside to check it out, and he must have run across a Seeker because it cut a long thin piece of skin off his arm and made him bleed, so Brandon ran into his house screaming and tried to wake his parents, but he was not able to find them.

He waited by the door all night and eventually fell asleep but when he awoke they were still missing.

Brandon stood and ran out of the house. When he reached the village square he saw a group of people crowding around something. That's when he found out that his parents were dead. So the Seekers must have killed them and infuriated Kevin."

Zak nodded. "Yea, that fits in the puzzle. After his killing spree around the world, Kevin sent the Seekers back to wherever it was George was hiding—"

Kami interrupted. "And that's when the Seekers came and put me and Brandon in the forest!"

Things were making sense, and hopefully they could help Brandon. Zak went on with his story, and Kami, especially, listened intently.

"Once they went back to the village that you and Brandon were in, things in Andren were quiet, but after about three days, Kevin was mad again and went on sending his Seekers after random people until the police found a weak spot in Kevin's mansion where few Seekers were. They went in, hard and heavy, bound and determined to capture Kevin.

"Kevin went down, along with all his Seekers, and this time Kevin had been sentenced a lifetime in jail at the age of twenty-seven in the most heavily guarded prison in Andren.

"As for the Seekers, they were caged again and put in a room completely isolated from everywhere on an island located in the middle of Lake Wendall. Both Kevin and the Seekers were held in captivity for eight years.

"Eight years later, the Seekers grew anxious in wanting to leave. Succeeding in breaking the bond of captivity, the Seekers were out and about. That's why Seekers are everywhere, but what we didn't know was that Kevin had escaped."

"And that must have been why Kevin went after Brandon, because Brandon is the son of George, and instead of watching his father suffer, he's making Brandon! It all makes sense!"

Kami rose, pacing around thinking the entire story over, making sure that she had it right. "There's one thing we still don't know. Why would Brandon come after me?"

An odd silence fell, but it was broken when Jon spoke, "Well, whatever it is, we need to find Kevin, and save Brandon."

Zak interrupted. "Kevin may still be back at the mansion, but the problem is that if Kevin learned from the past, he's going to have Seekers at every corner."

※※

Brandon's eyes slowly opened. At first things were blurry and mixed together, but his vision came back, only to see in front of him the mad man sitting in a chair. Brandon squirmed to the corner of the room and huddled into a ball like a beaten puppy, fearing that the man would call a Seeker into the room. But to his surprise, the man didn't. All he did was…just sit there. When suddenly the man looked up and spoke gently, "Go. I have no further use for you."

The man shoved his head into his hands. Brandon hesitated from his position and then bolted for the door, eyeballing the man along the way. Just as he reached about half the way to the door, Brandon stopped and thought for a moment. *What if this is a trick? What if it isn't? Freedom or beatings? Chance? Chance was one thing I haven't taken in a long time, taken a chance and just... well, winging it. Now is the perfect time, but I'm already beaten, and I can't afford another one.* Brandon then made his decision.

⁂

They were on the road again, on their way to Lenowa because they had to get certain supplies and then head over to Wenstal to climb the back cliff to the mansion.

Zak pulled the truck over to stop at a motel for the night in a city just outside Broad City. Everyone flew out of the cramped vehicle and into the building.

Once everyone was inside, someone checked them in. The clerk assigned them rooms and grabbed two room keys, handing them to Jon. Jon took the keys, and the clerk pointed to a hallway to his left. "Your rooms are ninety-seven and ninety-eight. Please enjoy your stay at the Mission Motel." The clerk placed his elbow on the desk in front of him and laid his head on top. The five grouped in line and walked down the hall. Just as they found their rooms Zak grabbed Jon by the shoulder and announced, "We're going to bring in the luggage. Be back in a second."

They turned around and walked off. Kami, Katherine, and Rachel opened the room ninety-seven and walked in. The room seemed a little older because of the worn-out wallpaper that was torn on certain edges; the furniture was a little battered down; the sheets on the bed were old and stained; and the kitchen, along with the appliances, were far from modern. Though it wasn't five stars, they were staying for only one night, and then they would check out the next morning and be on the road again.

The two boys came back with their hands full of luggage. As they walked in Johnny tripped on one of the bags that Zak carried and fell flat on his face, making a cry on the way down. "Oh crap!" When he climbed back up, he yelled at Zak. All Zak could do was bury his head into his hand and laugh.

Katherine and Rachel went and grabbed their luggage from the guys while Kami unlocked the guys' door. Just as Zak was going to give Rachel her suitcase, Jon accidentally hit Zak in the back of the knee, causing him to drop all the cases he had on Jon's foot. Jon then dropped all of the things *he* carried and yelled out while hopping on one foot and holding the one that was injured in the air. "Oh my gosh, what did you pack in these suitcases... *bricks?!*" At that point everyone stopped what they were doing and broke down laughing while Jon continued to hop around.

After everyone had settled in, with the guys and girls in their separate rooms, they all went to bed so that they could have an early rise in the morning. Everyone slept soundly except for one, Kami. She tossed and turned, trying to fall asleep, but couldn't; she was just so excited for the next day to come, a step closer to helping and seeing Brandon.

She slid up out of bed and started to walk around the room. After a couple times of aimlessly pacing around the room, she decided to take a walk in the motel. Kami slowly and quietly cracked open the front door, slipping out, hoping not to wake anyone. Once she had her body fully out, Kami tiptoed a few feet away from where her door was then she walked normal.

She wandered the few halls there were and repeated her route twice. On the third route around the small building, she stopped to get a small sip of water from the water fountain.

As she leaned down, her hair fell into her face and blocked all the things around her.

The moment after she finished, she looked back up and turned to the right to continue walking, but as she did, she saw a Seeker at the end of the hall.

It wasn't doing anything but just standing there. The eyes of the Seeker glowed brightly, and its nails were as long and sharp as ever. Kami reached for her whip; when she felt nothing, she realized that it was back in the room and mumbled under her breath, "Please God, don't let that *thing* step any closer."

Kami continued to eye the creature carefully, until it started to dissipate from the top down. That's when the blur appeared. As the Seeker was leaving, a thought ran through Kami's mind, *Should I go? Maybe it will take me to Brandon, but maybe not. Should I take the chance? What about Zak, Jon, Katherine, and Rachel? How will they know where I am? Now may be my only chance.* The Seeker was fully through, and now was time for Kami to make a huge decision, and quick.

⁂

"Did you honestly think that I would just let my revenge go and set you free? I mean really! Come on! Did you ever have a brain, or did I beat it to a pulp and you just can't think straight?" Kevin sighed to calm himself down. "You know I can't really call you all that stupid because, look at ya, if I were you, I would have left the person who was beating me."

"Why, you would have brought me back anyway!" The mad man raised the whip and released it against the throbbing bare back. Brandon cried out with tremendous pain as a whip crossed the middle of his back. Blood ran down not only his back, but his face and mouth from the punches and clawing that he had received earlier. And before that he was burned on the arm and dunked in a pool of water.

Brandon whimpered for a second as the mad man barked, "What did you tell Kami when you were out of my control!"

"N-nothing!" Brandon tried to yell back but failed in the attempt. The mad man shook his head in disbelief. "You know it's not good to lie." He raised up the whip and cracked it against the flesh on Brandon's back, peeling the dead skin from him to reveal bright red blood. Brandon yelped in pain as he tightened the muscles in his arms; Kevin had Brandon's arms tied around a pole, his wrists secured in thick leather wristbands. Every time Brandon fought against the leather, it would dig deep into his flesh, blistering along the way. He took in deep breaths to steady himself for the next swing. The mad man raised the whip in the air, ready to swing, and then he stopped. "You know how stupid you look right now, trying to protect your girlfriend when you know that I *will* find the truth."

Brandon closed his eyes tightly and answered. "Okay,

I told her a little about you and to tell Zak. That's it, I swear. Please no more beatings!"

Kevin dropped the whip and started to stroke his hand against his chin. "Huh, interesting... Your food will be here in a little while. And just to let you know, there was a minor malfunction in the system; that's why you were free for that moment. It won't happen again, so don't count on speaking with her anymore." He walked through the one door in the corner. Just as he did, a Seeker came in and threw a bowl full of ketesh in the middle of the floor (a mix of mashed peas, squash, beets, milk, a watery substance, and raw fish) then cut the bond that held Brandon to the pole, which he had just been beaten on, then carried it out of the room. Brandon fell to the ground, helplessly, and scurried to the only food he could have.

Once the Seeker left the room, a few seconds past, till in the opposite corner from the door a blur spun only to spit out Kami. Brandon paid no attention and just continued to eat thinking that it was a Seeker that lost its way. Kami stood up, looking around. She saw only one window that was up really high, letting in little light, the rest of the cell was almost black and the entire cell was made of bluish bricks, the floor and walls had bloodstains all over, and then she noticed that a human-shaped thing lay in the middle of the floor. It was hovering over something, making weird noises. Kami's curiosity grew as she started toward the thing. The closer she stepped, the less she heard from the creature and the more she noticed its disfigured body. She crept close enough to touch it, and when she did, the thing jumped a good inch or two in the air completely terrified.

Its face had blood all over it, a black eye, deep cuts, huge scratches, and long thin oily hair that drooped in its face. The body was so skinny, too skinny. It did have some fat, just not enough. Its ribs stuck out, and the stomach was pushed in under the middle of the ribs, sort of looking like it was sucking in but permanently. It wore a pair of baggy shorts that didn't really seem to fit, but no shirt. The entire middle section was bloody and full of whip marks. Its arms and legs looked like burned bones, barely any fat at all.

Kami bent down, horrified by the looks of the being. Her heart ached for all things she believed happened to the poor thing. She stared into the eyes of the scared struck animal, hoping to find out if it was a Seeker, but it wasn't. She saw that there was a soul in the being, and it was broken.

Kami spoke in a soft whisper. "My name is Kami. Who are you, and why are you here?"

The eyes of the being softened up from completely stiff to kind and gentle. The beaten *person* then started to speak in a torn whisper, "Is it really that bad that you can't tell who I am?"

Kami looked surprised as she studied him carefully then gasped, whispering his name. "Brandon? Oh my gosh, is that really you? What happened to you? Did that mad man do this?" Brandon pulled himself up with the little strength he had left to answer.

"Yea, it's me, and the mad man did do this. But how did *you* get here?"

"I was staying at a motel with the others, and I couldn't sleep, so I went on a walk around the building. A Seeker appeared, so when it left, I jumped into the blur. But all the other times I saw you, you weren't like this. How did this happen?" Just as Kami finished her last word, the two could hear footsteps coming toward the door. Kami panicked as she hid in a black corner, waiting to see what was going to happen next. Brandon went back to his original position, eating the little disturbing food that he received, when Kevin burst through the door.

"This thought has been bothering me ever since the incident happened. If the malfunction was minor, how were you staying out of control for so long?"

Brandon looked up from eating and answered quietly, "I don't know. It just happened."

Kevin placed his hand over his chin to think about how reasonable the answer sounded. He shrugged. "Well, they're on the move again. Except this time Kami seems to be gone."

The man seemed to be testing Brandon as he replied nervously, "So what now?"

"I don't know. Things aren't going according to plan. I mean that Seeker wasn't supposed to help Kami, much less be there. And she's not supposed to be here hiding in that corner." He turned swiftly, looking directly at her.

Kami about had a heart attack as she tried to stand. Her legs wobbled, and her skin turned pale. She had no weapon and no protection. Kevin walked up to her and grabbed her by the jaw. He held it tight, and Kami started to whimper, terrified. "How dumb do you think I am? Hiding in a corner and using one of my blurs to transport here! Seriously, I wasn't expecting you to be that plain dumb!" He stuck his face right in hers and started to spit. "And if you're going to try and tell me that Zak is going to show up and save the day, to try to get me to cower, you are sadly mistaken because I have Seekers everywhere that show me everything. All your little plans are ruined! How do you think I knew that you and the others were planning that trap to capture Brandon?"

Just then Kevin dropped Kami to the ground. Once she looked back at Kevin, she saw that Brandon had used all his strength to jump on his back. He pulled his arms around Kevin's neck and jolted back, choking the man. As Brandon continued, he tried to yell at Kami, "Go get out of here! Find a large green button outside the door, press it, and jump into the blur!"

"What about you?"

"Forget me, just go!" His grip loosened, Brandon, desperately holding on, yelled, "Get out of here!" Kami turned to the door, turning back to get one last glimpse at the man she loved. Her heart pounded with fear and worry the entire time.

Kami found the green button and slammed on it, hoping Brandon had the strength to kill the man. She didn't take her eyes off the door until the blur appeared. She waited a moment, believing Brandon would come through the door to go with her. The hole was starting to fade, and no one showed. She was about to jump in when the door opened, instead of Brandon, it turned out to be the mad man. Kami, without a second thought, dove in.

※※

The road blurred up again, and Kami flew out. She was outside the motel in the parking lot. Her heart ached at the thought of what Brandon must be going through for what he had done for her.

   She knew that she had to leave, but part of her wanted to stay and help him, maybe find a way out together, but things like that were just make-believe and only happened on cartoons. Kami pulled herself up and looked around when she noticed that Zak's truck was still parked in the same parking space. It was daylight out, and Kami remembered that she had just disappeared in the middle of the night, so she rushed to the motel building.

   Reaching the front door of the room that she had stayed in, Kami knocked on the door and waited for either Katherine or Rachel to answer. The second they did, the two screamed with joy, hugging her to where she nearly lost her breath. Hearing the screams, the guys came rushing out and saw that Kami returned.

   They settled down to find out where she had gone. "I know this will sound a little weird to you guys, but it really did happen, okay. Remember that as I tell the story, and I'm not making this up." Kami began, "I couldn't sleep, so I climbed out of bed and snuck out of the room, so I wouldn't wake anyone, to take a walk around the building. When I stopped at the water fountain, I saw a Seeker standing at the end of the hall, staring at me. After a couple seconds, the thing just left. So out of curiosity, I ran over to it and jumped in the blur it created."

   "At the time, did you have any questions or concerns about where that might take you?" asked Jon.

   "No, I really didn't. I just hoped that it would maybe take me to Brandon, and I knew that if it did and I didn't take the chance, then I would of missed the opportunity to possibly help him," answered Kami when Zak jumped in.

"Did you have anything to protect yourself with?" Kami looked down like a child telling her parent the bad thing she had just done.

"No."

Zak's face showed how peeved he was. "Why would you leave alone without your weapon?" He was starting to yell. "How could you be so irresponsible and stupid? Something could have hurt you or even killed you!"

Katherine stood up and tried to calm down Zak. She turned back around and told Kami to continue, so she did. "Well after that, I ended up in this dark cellar that had one tiny window, which let in very little light, and the whole place was just horrible. But in the middle of the floor was... Brandon, beaten and starved."

Kami started to tear up as she went on. "He looked terrible, just terrible. He was eating this horrible-looking and smelling thing, and his body was just so broken. Words can't even begin to describe what he looked like. When Kevin came in, I hid in this dark corner and waited as he questioned Brandon. But apparently he already knew about me since he spoke to me.

"He came closer; he grabbed my jaw and spat in my face. He even told me how Brandon knew about the plan we had to capture him. It was a Seeker hiding, taking the shape of something else—"

Rachel interrupted, "Wait, what? Why is Brandon like *that* then so mean and nasty and why is he like beaten then looking perfectly fine?"

"I don't know; I was about to ask him that, but that's when Kevin came in."

An odd silence fell upon the group. No one could answer the question. Not even Zak.

Then something else came up from what Kami had said about her experience with Brandon and Kevin, and that was how Kevin had said something about Seekers at every corner and that there was no way into the mansion. This was going to be a problem, and a huge one at that. The only thing that all five of them could think of was if all the cities and villages gathered their armies into one and caused a distraction, then the five could sneak into the mansion with ease. The plan sounded easy, but in reality, it really wasn't going to be. Not all the mayors would agree to do such a thing, especially not the mayor of Brownten.

"So what are we going to do?" asked Katherine.

"I don't know. Maybe we should try to convince everyone? It's worth a shot!" suggested Rachel.

Zak was leaning up against a wall looking at the floor when he suddenly leaped off and announced, "I know what we're going to do."

"We're going back to Broad City and convincing Carissa to get in on it, just like what Rachel said. But in order to get certain mayors to go along with it, you have to get their competition to agree, so that they feel compelled to follow, that way they don't look like cowards. Carissa, I know, will go along with it because Kevin was the one who sent the Seekers after her mother, so she'll get in on it for revenge.

"Then, after she's agreed, we go ask the mayor of Lenowa because Carissa and Maiya, the mayor of Lenowa, have always been in a competition to see who has the better city. So Maiya will feel like Carissa is showing off, and she won't like it, and she'll go along with it.

"After that, we'll go all the way back to Brownten and tell Nick about the other two, and knowing that there are already two in on it, he won't want to look bad. Lastly, we go to Wenstal, and you guys know that he'll join," explained Zak.

"Okay... and how do you know all this?" questioned Jon.

"Well, you know how I came from a rich family, right? Every time I went over to each city, these weaknesses would pretty much shine, because they would all talk about each other, and my parents told me so that when I grew up I could use the weaknesses to my advantage."

Everyone awed, and Zak's plan was going to be put into place.

⁂

Each person grew a little more cautious around people and other objects due to the last experience they had. They checked all their possessions and packed them away.

Instead of headed forward to Lenowa, Zak turned the truck around and headed back toward Broad City.

On the trip back, Jon decided to try and be a comedian and started telling jokes. "What does a diamond become when it is placed in water?"

Everyone sighed, and Johnny blurted out the answer. "Wet!" He laughed a little, then saw that no one else was, so he came up with a riddle. "Okay, if you guys don't like my jokes, then here's a riddle. A murderer is sentenced to death and has the opportunity to choose what his death sentence will be. His three options are, one, he can be thrown into raging fires; two, be put in a room with assassins that have loaded guns; or three, be tossed into a room with lions that haven't eaten in three years. Which room is the safest?"

"Jon, that's the dumbest riddle I think that I have ever heard in my life," expressed Zak as he drove.

Jon looked at him. "If you think that it's so stupid, then what is the answer, smart one?"

"The lions. They haven't eaten in three years; they'd be dead."

Jon looked dumbfounded as he turned to face the windshield. "Man, you got that fast!"

※-※

It had been five days and five nights of traveling. They were just finishing the sixth day when they finally came close to the gate of Broad City.

As they passed by the same green grass and same roads, Kami stared out the window, thinking about the experience she had just had. *What if he would have made it through the blur with me? What if he would have made it through with me in the first place? If he did, would we still be chased? What is making him act like that? And why were all those scars there then, but then gone when he confronts us? What could make that happen?*

"Kami... Kami! Kami!"

Kami shook her head and turned toward the person who called her name and asked, "What?"

"Dude, we're here! Now get out of the truck!" announced Rachel. Kami looked out the window and saw the magnificent city. She opened the door and jumped. They were back in Broad City and in the parking lot in front of the city hall.

After gathering everyone around in a circle behind the truck, Zak started to speak. "Okay you guys. We're here, and we need to do the same as last time because this plan won't work unless it's worded correctly. No one speaks unless spoken to, okay?" Everyone nodded, and they started up the stairs into the city hall.

They walked straight into the mayor's office, sort of in a hurry, but when they did, they saw Brandon, holding a blade to the mayor's throat. Brandon looked up and saw the five standing there, staring. "Aw, we have company. How wonderful!"

Brandon put his blade away and walked beside the fear-stricken mayor. "Take one step, and she dies. The only one who can move is Kami, and she needs to stand in the middle of the room." Zak looked at her and nudged her forward. Kami slowly walked into the position Brandon wanted her in, standing there gripping her necklace. "So, you found your way into the mansion and saw your boyfriend... Oh wait that was me, wasn't it?"

He started laughing when Kami interrupted him and corrected, "No, that wasn't you."

"Oh, it wasn't? Well, you can believe what you want to, and since your friends are here I think that now would be a great time to... kill them." Brandon announced sarcastically as he pulled out both of his blades and just held them. "I feel like being nice today. Carissa, tell the people of your city to stay inside so that none of them get hurt during the battle... now!" barked Brandon.

Carissa turned to the speaker, switching it on,

speaking frantically into the microphone. "Attention, attention to all inhabitants of Broad City. Return to your houses now. This is an emergency. Get to your homes now! This is not a drill!" Carissa pulled her finger off the button and turned to face the scene.

"Good, after about ten minutes, the battle will start. Kami, get back with your group."

Brandon led everyone to the middle of the city, into an intersection. Five against one; it wasn't a fair fight. Brandon stood on one side of the intersection and the five on the other side. Brandon tied his robe together and put his hood on, while the others reached for their weapons.

Once both sides were ready, Brandon then cried out, "Come at me with all you have!"

The five did as they were told. All at once the five charged at him, full force and speed. When they tried to hit him, Brandon blocked all attempts and flung each to the side. It seemed as though he learned the technique each person used and predicted their next move.

Zak was the first up. He jumped into the air with his blade ready to strike Brandon in half. Instead Brandon met blade to blade with Zak and shoved him back. Zak landed on his feet and charged at Brandon. Zak swung his blade across the middle, but Brandon ducked and took a shot at Zak's legs. Responding to the attempt, Zak leaped into the air, flipping backwards; he landed on his feet but knelt down. Then Jon leaped over Zak like they would in leapfrog then ran at Brandon, he swung his elbow into the air and tried to strike, but Brandon jumped to the side, and Jon hit the floor. Recovering from the miss, Jon ran back at Brandon and tried to strike.

Katherine and Rachel both ran at him with full speed. Katherine threw three daggers, and Rachel threw her spear at Brandon. But instead of getting hit, Brandon formed an x with his blades and broke it to deflect the objects. Kami pushed the button on the whip, forcing the chain out. She ran forward and slung her weapon with rage at the impersonator. As Kami ran forward, her whip swung to the side, gaining speed for a powerful strike. When she threw the end of the whip at him, Brandon dodged and rolled to the side toward Jon.

Seeing Brandon come at him, Jon leaped at Brandon. Once out of the roll, Brandon dove underneath the leap, and landed flat on his stomach. Zak came in front of Brandon and went to strike. Instead of a miss, Zak sliced down Brandon's arm as he tried to get up.

Jon came from behind as Brandon fought Zak. He chopped the robe Brandon was wearing in half and skidded his blade across Brandon's back. Brandon's blade disappeared into the air, and Brandon fell to the ground. Watching the blades dissipate, Zak turned around to see if the torn robe was still there, but it wasn't.

As Brandon lay there, Jon bent down to examine him, but when he did, the body burst into the air, having dust fill the air. When it receded, Brandon was gone, and a Seeker lay in his place, staring at them.

Jon quickly killed the Seeker and turned to the others. "So was that him in the beginning or just a Seeker?"

No one except Kami could really answer, but when she did, she said that she didn't know. "I couldn't tell if that was him or not. When I looked into his eyes, it seemed like a mix, as if he had a soul, but at the same time didn't."

"Just forget about it" spoke Zak seriously as he walked toward city hall. *If that was really him in the beginning how did he switch to the Seeker in the middle of the battle?*

The five walked back to the city hall, and in the office, Carissa was on the speaker "Citizens of Broad City, the battle is over, but please remain in your homes until further notice." Zak looked at Carissa.

"I know that this is a bad time, but we need your help…We believe that Kevin has escaped from prison, and we also believe that the person you just saw is being controlled, somehow, by him, and we will need your help to stop him."

"What! Kevin hasn't escaped. If he did, the prison would have announced it."

"You're forgetting that he is the one who controls the Seekers, and they may be taking his place in the prison!"

"Well, we still don't know that for a fact. What do you need?"

"All I need is for a part of your army to be ready so that when we call you, they might be able to make a distraction, to drive the Seekers at Kevin's mansion away so that we can get in and rescue the guy that you just saw."

"That Brandon guy? Who is he, and why do you want to rescue him?"

"We want to rescue him because of this girl here." Zak grabbed Kami and continued. "That is her lifelong friend. And if you saw what he's been through, you'd want to help him."

"He didn't look that beat up to me."

"We can't explain that right now! We still need your help to take Kevin down. Will you help?"

"Well... I don't know..." Carissa paused. She walked over to her desk and sat down in her chair. "It would be a very big risk to take... Have you asked any others?" Zak paused for a second before answering, caught off guard by the question.

"Well, no, not yet. But after this, we're heading over to Lenowa."

"So you're going to ask Maiya, huh?" The mayor turned her chair around and faced the opposite direction and whispered to herself, "This could prove to everyone that I'm a better mayor, and if we win, I would be able to use this on the next election!" Carissa flew her chair around and announced her decision. "Okay, I will aid in the distraction. How many troops will you need?"

"I'm not quite sure, but once we've contacted everyone, we will let you know," assured Zak as the mayor nodded and went back to her computer.

Jon, Katherine, Kami, and Rachel had walked out and were heading for the truck when the mayor looked up and saw that Zak was just about to leave through the doorway.

"Zak? Zak, wait..."

Zak stopped and peeked around the doorway, "What?"

"Thanks for showing when you did... If you guys hadn't shown... the good Lord only knows what would have happened."

"God has his ways of making miracles happen, and I guess that was one of yours."

10

They were on the road again, heading for Lenowa to see the mayor, Maiya. In the truck the five goofed off and joked about odd things just for the heck of it. "Okay, what did the little rose say to the big rose?" asked Jon, trying to keep the secret as they all asked, "What?"

"Hi, bud!" Jon burst out laughing, but no one seemed to get it. When Jon stopped he looked up and exclaimed, "Wow, you guys are a horrible crowd. The rose is a rose 'bud,' and it says, 'Hi, bud…'" They all stared at him blankly, and he just shook his head in disappointment. "Never mind. Wait maybe you'll get this one. Okay, get ready 'cause it's going to be amazing. Ready? What is the difference between roast beef and pea soup?" No one answered, and Jon held in the laugh from bursting out as he answered the question, "You can roast beef, but you can't *pee* soup!" Johnny broke down laughing as the others just shook their heads at the bad joke. "Don't you guys get it? Man, you people are not the brightest! Worst crowd *ever!*" announced Jon still laughing. "Man, I crack myself up!"

The trip continued on for the next week, making it a year and two weeks since Kami met the other four.

<hr>

As they pulled up to the huge gate that guarded the city, Jon had a bad feeling that something very terrible happened behind the grand gate.

Sometimes Jon received feelings that told him something bad was going to happen or it had already happened. He wasn't always right, but most of the time, he had it right on the nail. If Jon's feeling had truth to it, and something bad had happened or might happen, then the five might be able to help those living in the city.

They all decided that it would be best to have a look around and warn the mayor that something terrible could happen really soon.

Zak and Jon leaped out of the truck to punch in the password needed for this gate, to open the door. Once the code was entered, the large gate opened in front on them to reveal a city that looked like a bomb exploded on it. Grey dust shot out, creating a cloud around them. Zak and Jon covered their faces, trying to hold back their coughs and jumped back into the truck. The dust remained too thick to see through for a few minutes. Once it thinned out, Zak started to drive around the broken city.

Few buildings were standing in the city of Lenowa, and the ones that were standing had huge chunks missing and cars blown into the sides. It seemed more dull and dark the further they traveled. The color of the city seemed drained, leaving only dull, ugly colors. A mix of dust and fog gathered in the air. Trees had tumbled over cars, houses, parks, and many other buildings. The streets overlapped other broken parts while random objects were blown across it.

As they looked around, they noticed that there wasn't anyone around. Things were very suspicious. Was it an attack by the Seekers? Many questions could be asked, but they all came down to the one thing that summarized them. *Why aren't there any corpses?*

There was no way to tell when the Seekers were going to attack, so it had to of have been a surprise. Same with the weather. The gang drove around and around seeing more and more damages but still no people.

They were reaching the end of the city when Katherine looked out her window to see a gigantic pile. "Hey, Zak, pull over to the left, in the park. See that enormous pile-type thing?"

"Yea," he replied as he did so. When they moved closer, they could make out that the pile contained the dead corpses of the inhabitants. The three girls gasped with shock as they covered their mouths.

"Oh my gosh, this is horrible!" exclaimed Rachel, with the other two nodding their heads in agreement.

Zak and Jon walked up closer to see how a few of them had died. It seemed as if the people were slaughtered then burned. When they checked other corpses, a loud crushing noise echoed throughout the entire city.

A few seconds passed, and another loud crash-type noise echoed. The five looked around then at each other. The loud noise happened more and more frequently, and it seemed to be moving closer. What could have killed all of these people and was now making these noises? The thought ran circles in their heads when the word

"Seekers" popped up in their minds. *Was it all the Seekers, or was it Brandon too? How many could be here? Are we sure that it was them? What else is there? Nothing. It has to be the Seekers. Why attack here? There's nothing here, just, poor merchants and middle-class families.*

The five grouped together as they reached for their weapons, preparing themselves for what lay ahead. They formed a circle, facing all directions. As the noises crept closer, the ground started to shake harder. Closer and closer, they came until it sounded as if "it" was right in front of them. The noises just then stopped. A brief silence lay upon them. Sweat dripped from their faces, scared to death of the next move. Jon started to pray aloud, asking God that he would please watch over them and keep them safe. The others listened and prayed the same thing. When they opened their eyes and looked forward, in front of Jon was a building that shook violently.

Jon stared as the others formed a line beside him. The building slid off the foundation and onto the ground to reveal an entire army of thousands upon thousands of Seekers staring back at them with their bright red eyes. There was no sign of Brandon.

11

The Seekers marched forward

at a medium pace. Stunned, the five watched and waited. They held their weapons tightly. The closer the Seekers limped forward, the faster their hearts thrashed around in their chest. When suddenly an idea popped up in Kami's head. "Zak, would we be able to get into the truck and drive off?"

"I don't know, from the looks of it, we're surrounded by thousands of Seekers, but it's worth a try." Though he was nervous, Zak kept his cool by directing the others. "Guys, we all need to run back to the truck and fast." The others nodded, and they turned around and ran as fast as they could to the grayish truck.

Seeing the five run for the truck, the Seekers sped up their pace, switching it to a limping sprint.

Swinging the door open, Rachel crawled in and onto the other side. Next in line for the back was Kami, and she slid in. Lastly was Katherine. Once she was in, Zak and Jon leaped into the two front seats. Zak pulled out his keys from his pocket and jammed the truck key into the ignition then tried to start the truck, while Jon locked all the doors and doubled checked them.

Everything was going good, the truck started, and they were still living, but one last problem stood in their way, the fact that thousands of Seekers were now piled up on top of the truck trying to claw their way in. The screeches of the nails digging down the window and through the metal from the rest of the vehicle hurt everyone's ears. So many Seekers were on top of the truck, if they were to look out the window all they would be able to see was the rough dark green skin and a few gleaming red eyes. There was nothing that could be done; they were trapped, and unless a miracle happened the five were done for.

It felt like hours went by, but instead it was just ten long and miserable minutes of chaos. The Seekers were breaking through; the glass wasn't going to hold out for much longer. Hands were already peeking in trying to hit them. Rachel and Katherine pulled out their weapons and started fighting back, swinging at any hand that came near them. Every time one of the two sliced a Seeker's hand off, the hand would contribute to the pile.

Jon and Zak did the same, except what they were doing was taking the dead hands and fighting back with *their* nails and shoving them out of the holes. In each of their minds, a prayer of help was being said.

Finally, the glass gave in and completely shattered, and the Seekers flooded into the cramped truck, their nails scratched the five and tore strand after strand of skin. Blood spilled on everything and cries from the girls could be heard from miles away. Zak and Jon tried to fight back, but there were just too many Seekers peeling skin and knocking the weapons out of their hands. All hope just seemed lost; there was nothing that could be done.

12

"Please, call off the Seekers! Stop doing this to them!" cried out Brandon, chained to the wall.

"Do you think that I would stop this after you doing what you did? How dare you!" yelled back the mad man as he gave a signal to the Seeker in the back corner of the cell. The Seeker walked over to Brandon and lifted up his legs and pulled. Brandon howled with pain and suffering; his limbs felt like they were tearing off, tendon by tendon.

When Kevin gave another signal, the Seeker put Brandon back on the ground. Losing his balance, due to the pain all throughout his legs, Brandon fell onto his knees. He breathed heavily, trying to handle the ache.

"Now look at the TV!" barked the mad man. Brandon lifted his head to look at the portable television. In front of him, he saw the truck being invaded by mounds of Seekers. He heard the cries of terror as the monsters crawled in. His heart ached with sorrow as he continued to watch, knowing that there was nothing he could do. He'd take a million more beatings just to keep them safe. Kevin looked down at Brandon, mocking him as he spoke. "Too bad you can't do anything! They were trying so hard to find you, and that, that is what looking for you brought them."

"Why don't you just kill me now? You've already had me here for forever and done everything to me!" He was now trying to yell, but instead of a yell, it was more of a loud deformed whisper. "You've made her suffer, and them too. You've beaten me many times with whips, canes, nails, punches, nearly suffocated me by dunking me under water, choked me, starved me, and burned me, forcing me to eat the most foul things, and not to mention that you've gotten me to almost kill all of them. What more do you think it will take to torture me enough that you finally get bored and kill me?!"

Kevin knelt down and gripped Brandon's chin. "I'll be done with you when they finally decide to show up, but until then we're going to have way more fun than before."

<hr />

"Zak, what are we going to do?" screamed Kami as she fought back against all the Seekers in the back seat.

"I...I don't know!" replied Zak as he shoved a Seeker out the window. "Get out of the truck. Fight your way through and run!" suggested Zak as he did just that, with the others following.

As they kicked the door open, Katherine, Rachel, and Kami charged out into the crowd, striking anything that came in their way. As for Jon, he jumped through the window and climbed onto the top of the truck, stepping on the Seekers below. Once up there, he saw that Zak was working on clearing it. "Looks like you could use a hand?" asked Jon as he slit a Seeker in the back of the neck, making it dissipate into the air.

"Naw, fighting thousands of monsters is just what I like to do in my free time!" yelled back Zak sarcastically, pinning a Seeker to the ground, stabbing it in the chest.

The three girls tried staying together, but ended up separated when swarms of Seekers came along attacking them here and there.

"Katherine? Kami? Where are you guys?" wondered Rachel, when a Seeker popped up in front of her. She hit the Seeker across the face with the spear and kicked it into the others behind it. Rachel looked around and tried to stab the Seekers all around her.

"Rachel? Kami? Where'd you go?" screamed Katherine as she fought against the Seekers around her. Stabbing all that came within spitting distance. She turned around and threw a knife into a Seeker's red eye then flipped toward it to retrieve the knife, sliding it out of the eye through the skin, to hit others.

"Jon? Jon is that you?" Jon looked over and saw Kami fighting a Seeker off to the side. He shoved the Seeker he was battling back and jammed the end of his weapon in its gut; he then ran toward her.

When he reached closer, he saw that a Seeker was running behind Kami, aiming right for the heart. Jon sped up his pace and screamed at Kami, "Get out of the way! Look behind you!"

Kami couldn't understand the mixed slurred words; she knocked a Seeker back as another came at her. "What?"

He started to gesture his hands, to get her to move. She didn't look at him; instead she battled the two Seekers that were knifing at her.

Once he was close enough he made a choice, Jon sliced through her opponents and knocked Kami backwards to the ground, but before Jon could strike the last seeker, it charged its knives through his heart. The strong force of the impact caused Jon's head to fling back as he let out a grunt. A few other Seekers looked up and immediately charged at the body. Laying underneath, Kami tried to move and help, but the Seeker that should have knifed her was holding her in between its feet. "No, stop! Jon!" screamed Kami, thrashing around trying her hardest to stop the Seekers.

They jerked their knives up to remove them from Jon's chest, then the first Seeker to stab Jon let out a wail, and the entire army dissipated into the air. Once all of the Seekers fled, Jon dropped to the ground, gasping for breath; they had charged him in the heart and lungs. His eyes were wide, tears built up and climbed down his cheeks, and muscles loosened as he lost control of his body.

13

"No, no! Why...why did you have to...?" Kami scrambled to Jon's side, tears dangling from her chin; she picked his head up off the floor and looked into his eyes, brushing his hair back gently.

"Pl-please help-help Brandon, and..." Jon stopped for a moment to struggle for a breath of air then continued. "Give...give him a...a huge...cheeseburger for me..." He struggled to get the words out. "Also...tell...Zak that...I'm going...to...miss...him."

Jon's head then felt lighter as it fell to the side, lifelessly. There was no bringing him back. He was dead. Johnny "Jon" Tenoria was dead.

"Why didn't you just let me get hit!? Why couldn't I have just understood what you were trying to tell me!?" screamed Kami.

By now Zak, Katherine, and Rachel started toward the two. When they saw what had happened, tears poured from the girls' eyes and they turned away. Zak knelt down beside Jon, heartbroken, and Kami scooted away.

"Hey, buddy..." He held Jon's lifeless body in his arms, his eyes turned red, and his face turned pale with disbelief.

Zak's tough hard face tore away into one that was shattered and destroyed. "You can't, just can't leave me here with these girls. You know that I've never been…been good with bein' soft…Jon…Jon…do you remember the time when we first met the girls…? You…you were trying to be smooth…but instead…you looked like such a…a…goof ball…but now look…You went out with both…getting a better score than me. Man, I'm gonna miss ya…Life won't ever be the same…Oh, Jon, why?" Zak pulled Jon's body up to his and hugged him, long and hard; his eyes and face tightened. Refusing to let him go, Zak clenched his fists tight against Jon's back. "I promise that Kevin will pay for all the pain he has put upon everyone." Then something happened, something that not even Jon had witnessed before, and that was to see…Zak shed a single tear.

14

They were on the road again, it was silent, and no one was willing to try and lift the mood, that job belonged to Jon. It had already been three days since the death; they stayed in the city for those three days to mourn him. But the pain was still glued on everyone in their hearts; no matter how much it hurt, there was no pulling it off.

Zak was the one who was hurt the most though. No one had known, or been friends with him as long as Zak. He was also the one who was closest to Jon. They were like brothers. Zak always protected and looked out for him. The two practically grew up together. Getting into all kinds of trouble, blaming each other so they wouldn't get punished, and having competitions to see who could date the most girls were just some of the things they did together. When Zak said that life was never going to be the same, he was telling the truth. Memories suddenly started to come back to him, all of Jon.

"Zak… stop looking for Brandon…" told Kami in a low, depressed tone as she looked out the window, but Zak corrected her still facing up front.

"No... I made a promise to you, and I intend to keep it. But Katherine, Rachel, I want you guys to stay at home..." Zak took a pause; it sounded as if he was trying to control his tears and then continued, "I... I want you to stay 'cause I don't want you guys to get hurt... not like... you know..."

Katherine and Rachel nodded. "Yea... we understand." They turned to Kami. "Sorry for, you know, having to leave and all, but..."

"I know. I don't even know if I want to continue..." She turned her head to look out the window. "I know that it sounds horrible, knowing what he's going through, but... he might be dead, and... I just... just can't see myself going on... this search without him."

"Yea, we understand; it's the same with us," agreed Katherine.

"Hey, guys... just please..." Zak paused for a sec. "Please stop... stop talking... about it... What's done is done... There's no changing it."

※─※

Once they reached Andren four days later, Zak dropped off Rachel and Katherine at the house and packed a few extra things. He packed it all into the truck but then decided to stay the night or two, just to get a little more rest and recover from the loss. Kami agreed, and they made it happen.

What was supposed to be just two days turned into weeks, and those weeks turned into two months. During this time, nothing happened, just grieving for the loss. It was just so hard to move on, especially for Zak. He just stayed in his room, only coming out to eat; that was all. There was already a bathroom in his room and a bed and everything that he needed. The few times he did come out were to eat, and even then it was fast, five minutes at the most, then it was back to the room. Every time someone tried to talk to him, he just answered back with "hm," or a "k," or if they were lucky, it was a "yea"; never was it happy or cheery. The words had a depressed, low, soft tone to them. Katherine, Rachel, and Kami were all sad too, but Zak had been hit the worst.

They all were worried about him; things seemed like he went into a great depression. If so, he'd really need to see a doctor, but still, it was all just a thought. At least that's what they thought.

Things were okay, a little scary, at first, but then they started to worsen over time. First Zak wouldn't even talk when he was asked a question; it seemed as though he just didn't hear the question, instead of just ignoring them. Second, he quit eating, wouldn't even come out of his room. Katherine knocked on the door, asking if he was okay, but there was no answer. And third, all movement that could be heard behind the door stopped.

Everything had happened over a long period of time, and the worrying grew each and every day. Katherine had Rachel and Kami behind her and started to knock... no answer. So in response, Katherine reached for the knob on the door and twisted it. Locked. She tried to bust the door down, but no luck, it was way too hard. Rachel and Kami joined in and started to run against the door with all of their might. Still, no luck. Even the three combined weren't that strong; they were weak when it came to this; and plus it hurt their shoulders, so they stopped.

"What are we going to do?" asked Kami.

"I'm not sure," responded Rachel. "Wait, what if we bought something like a ram and shoved it against the door?"

"Yea, Rachel... that's a great idea, I'll just run down to the store and go buy a ram," Katherine replied sarcastically, and Rachel gave Katherine "the look."

"The look" is an evil look that both of them knew and used to show if they were mad, frustrated, or annoyed with someone.

"Well... there's not that many—. Wait, isn't there a window in his room?" questioned Rachel. Katherine looked up at her.

"Yea, Yea there is. I think I know where you're going with this."

"Yea, why don't we pick the lock on the window and get in through there!"

"About time you come up with a good idea!"

"Hey, I didn't hear you throwing any ideas out there!"

"Oh hush," joked Katherine as she led the way outside.

Arriving outside, they sneaked around the house and through the bushes with thorns that bordered it. "Ouch, stupid thorns!"

"Kami, be quiet!" urged Rachel as they continued to the window.

"It's a good thing that this house isn't a two story!" whispered Katherine.

As they reached the window, they saw that Zak was just sitting in a chair, staring at a wall in a corner. He was slouched down in a chair, his legs were wide apart with his feet flat on the ground, and his arms dangled at his sides.

"Wow, I know that we can be boring but not to the point where this happens!" exclaimed Kami. Zak moved his head as if he heard. The three dropped down to the ground, so that they couldn't be seen.

Rachel and Katherine both looked at Kami. "Be quiet!"

Kami shrugged her shoulders and mouthed the word "sorry." They slowly stretched back up toward the window to peek through. But when they did, they saw in front of them, Zak staring back with possessed-looking eyes. He had his blade next to the window, pressing it up to the glass as if he were going to jam it through and kill one of them. The girls screamed as loud as they could and jumped back, rolling over the bushes.

All three, finally slid over the bushes and started sprinting toward downtown, fearing what would happen if they were to go back into the house. As they ran, Rachel turned to Katherine, who was in the middle. "Where are we going?"

"To the hospital!"

"Why to the hospital?" asked Kami.

"Because there is something big time wrong with Zak, and we need help!"

"I agree, but how are *they* going to help?" questioned Rachel.

"We'll also need to get the police!"

15

The three walked into the police station and stood in front of a man in a navy blue uniform. He was reading a magazine about how to attract women. "Excuse me," began Katherine. The man lowered the magazine. "Hi. Sorry to bug you, but we need the police... right away."

"Okay, why do you need us?"

"It's my friend, he's... well... not himself, and it's more like a great depression."

"Okay, so why do you need our help?"

"My friend could potentially get violent and start doing things that could end up like... Kevin Beraldi." The man's eyes grew to the size of footballs, and he leaned forward.

"Who is your friend?"

"Zak Delltoria."

"Well, this isn't good!"

"Yea, we lost Jon in a battle, and he's taken it really hard."

"Okay, I'll get a squad on it right away! You also might want stop by the hospital."

"Yea, that's where we're headed next!"

"When and where should the squad meet you?"

Katherine looked at Rachel, Rachel then whispered into her ear. Katherine looked up and answered. "At the front doors of the hospital at around six."

"Alright, they'll be there."

※—※

In the meantime, the three caught a ride in a cab to the hospital. They leaped out of the cab, throwing whatever money they had into the front on their way out.

Charging through the many different halls and almost running into many people, they finally reached the chief of staff. "Excuse me." Katherine started tapping the man's shoulders. "Um, I'm sorry to bother you, but I need a doctor right away." The man turned around, looking tired and just wanting to go home; he wore a white lab coat with a blue shirt underneath and jeans.

"Okay, what do you need?"

"It's my friend; he could potentially end up like Kevin Beraldi."

The man's eyes went from almost shut to wide open in a heartbeat. "I'll get a team right on it in like two minutes. Just wait a sec."

Katherine nodded "Oh, and we've already contacted the police!"

"Good," replied the doctor as he jogged off.

After about two minutes, like the doctor said, he had a team already to go. "Okay, the police should be outside the hospital by now, so let's go," announced Rachel as she, Katherine, and Kami led everyone out.

Once outside and in the canopy, they saw a huge team prepared and ready. The doctor then turned to Katherine and whispered, "Why so many cops?"

"Oh, I forgot to mention that the patient is... Zak Delltoria."

"Okay, I see why now!"

Zak was a pretty famous guy; everyone knew who he was and how good he was with his weapon. He had once helped the city through the time when Kevin sent Seekers to destroy Andren. He also was a given key to the city and dropped college to help protect and defend the city from any danger. At the age of fifteen, Zak led people from buildings, parks, and homes out of the city when the Seekers attacked. He also stayed behind after everyone left to help take out the Seekers one by one and retake the city. But the thing he was most known for was his life-risking action of running into a burning building, which was close to collapsing and crawling with Seekers, to save the lives of four small children.

"Okay, people, how are we going to do this?" asked Katherine when the chief of police stepped in.

"Here are the schematics to the house." One of the cops set up a table, and the chief laid down the piece of paper.

"His room is here," pointed Rachel.

"Okay, so we're going to need to come around here and here to ensure that he doesn't run out," started the chief. "But if he attacks..."

"We'll handle him," Katherine spoke up nervously. "We know his moves, and he wouldn't dare try and kill us... Th-that's why he didn't stab his blade into one of us in the window." Rachel and Kami looked up at Katherine.

"Are you sure about that? He's not himself and might not think about if it's us or not. I mean, we couldn't even bust a door down! Much less take down Zak," exclaimed Kami.

"Rachel and I can fight; he wouldn't hurt any of us... but the cops, maybe."

"Well, guess that's the plan. Are you sure that he could be like Kevin?" questioned the chief.

Katherine looked up. "Yea, there's no doubt about it."

16

"What's wrong with Zak?" asked Brandon lowly. Kevin looked down at the boy.

"He's going through what I did. He lost someone... someone he cared for... the only person that really knew him... And with that one person gone, he knows he has nothing to live for..."

"Just because that's the way you felt, doesn't mean that he feels that same way!" shouted Brandon, Kevin chuckled at the theory and kicked Brandon, who now was chained to the lower part of the wall, across the face, hard. Brandon's head bobbled a moment then went back to watching the portable, just like he was used to it. "Why did you have to kill Jon?" yelled Brandon.

"Well, I didn't command the Seekers to; they just did. I can't keep them under control forever. I have to let them out, off the leash sometimes, but I did send them to go and attack the five."

Brandon looked down and away then whispered to himself. "All this just to come help me... me, of all people. Why? Why did *he* have to die?"

The police split into three groups, one for the back, another for the left, and the last for the right. As for the doctors, they stood out front, waiting for the coast to be clear. Kami, Katherine, and Rachel each split up too. Kami to the back, Katherine to the left, and Rachel to the right.

Stepping quietly through the cut grass, the groups moved closer and closer to the normal house.

Fear struck each and every soul with each step. After seeing what Kevin was able to pull off, only the good Lord could see what a skilled warrior would do.

In the back, things were going great; they were able to reach the house and look through the living room window, and nothing was there. For the left, same thing, going great. The team reached the window to the kitchen and was sneaking in.

As for the right, they had the tougher task, sneaking in through Kami's room, which was right next to Zak's. They had to be extra silent and move swifter than the rest or else. God only knew what would happen.

Hearts of the ones next to them could be heard, and sweat glided down from the cheeks of the men. One thought ran through the minds of all, *what if Zak hears us coming in?* Though it sounded unlikely that so many could be scared of one, it was something that couldn't be helped.

Zak's parents were rich, and Zak pretty much received whatever he wanted, and what he wanted was to learn how to wield a blade. His parents hired the best teacher that they could find, and Zak took in all that he was taught. Learning quickly was a gift for him; he handled the blade with ease and glided the blade through the air swiftly and gracefully. Though he was at a young age, Zak matured fast and grew into the man he was today. Having all this knowledge on his weapon and how to handle it was something to be feared.

All three groups were now inside the house, tiptoeing through the halls; they all met up together in the middle of the living room and stared at their destination.

Getting in front of the door, the four biggest policemen stepped by the door and counted to three. On three, the men turned to the door and kicked it. But instead of it opening, the door remained closed, and the men turned around holding their legs mouthing the word "Ouch!" Everyone jumped and looked at the door wide eyed, hoping that Zak wouldn't come out.

"Sorry, Kami was trying to get her shoes on and accidentally tripped," announced Katherine, making an excuse for the noise, but there was no reply.

"Yea, sorry. It was my fault," apologized Kami, going along with what Katherine was doing.

One thought came to mind after this, *how could this door withstand four men built like a tree?*

"How is that door withstanding those kicks?" asked Brandon softly, yet with shock.

"Well, when the girls were in their rooms, before they had tried to *get* in his room, I sent a Seeker or two over there to paste themselves on the door as a clear hard substance, so that Zak could sulk, and feel worse day after day until I see that he has lost his mind, then I would go down there myself and convince him to join me in having revenge against you."

"You really are messed up in the head."

Kevin looked at Brandon and laughed. "Wow, you think that I'm messed up? You're chained to a wall, getting different ways of torture, and you keep smarting off to the one in charge of it all?" He laughed again then continued. "If I were you, I would shut my mouth and keep it shut."

"Why?"

"*Why?* What do you mean *why?*"

"Why would I want to shut my mouth?"

"Are you stupid?"

"Maybe. It's possible that you've beaten my brain into a smoothie of brain juice."

"What?"

"What is *what?* Why do we use the word *what* when we could say something else? What do you think could have happened?"

"Uh, I guess that's possible, but…"

"But *what?*"

"But still why wouldn't you want to shut your mouth?"

"Are *you* stupid?"

"No."

"Are you sure about that? 'Cause you use the word *what.*"

"Y-yes."

"Well then okay."

"Then okay what?"

"What?"

"What?"

"I don't know. You said, 'What?' I didn't say anything."
"Yes, you did."
"*No,* I didn't."
"Yes, you did. Wait; didn't you?"
"No."
"No, you didn't say anything, or no, you said something."
"What are you talking about?"
"I don't know!"
"Okay."
"Then okay what?"
"*What* is *what* when *what* is used in a sentence like 'Then okay what?' And why would you want to say, 'Remove yourself from the door'?"
"What? Why would I want to say that?"
"That's what I asked you! And ha, I made you to say *what* so in order to make the *what* go away, just say it, and it will all make sense, 'cause then all the *whats* and brain talk and stupidity will be gone!"
"Okay...? Remove yourself from the door. There I said..." Kevin shook his head and cleared his mind of all the nonsense that he had just been through and realized what he had just said. He turned to the television and saw a blur happen then disappear.

※—※

"Whoa, what happened?" whispered Kami, shocked, as she turned from the door.
"What was what?" asked the chief of police. "The door...like a blur just happened on it and went away!"
"What do you think it was?"

"I don't know? Maybe a Seeker? Try kicking the door down again!"

"Okay..." The chief turned to the men who did the first kicks and told them to try again. Everyone placed themselves back into their positions and waited. The four men steadied and went to kick as hard as they could.

They sent the door flying, knocking it across the room and against the bed on the other side. The cops swarmed the room, their guns close and cocked, ready to use them just in case they would ever *need* to be used. After all were through the door, Katherine, Rachel, and Kami walked in. Everything looked normal; the bed made, floor cleaned, desk arranged, everything perfectly fine... except in the left corner they saw Zak sitting in the same chair he had been in since the last time they saw him in the window. He didn't move, speak, or look at who just burst through the door.

Katherine walked closer to Zak speaking softly. "Zak... Zak, Rachel, Kami, and I are really worried about you; will you please just come out of this room and talk to us?" Zak continued to stare at the wall in front of him, acting as if he never heard her. "Zak, please, you're really scaring me. Please stop. We can get through this together, little by little."

"I'm not a kid... so stop treating me like one, and get these cops out of my house!" Zak still didn't move, just yelled, but at least he spoke.

"No, they're not going to leave until..."

"Until what?" He spun around, staring coldly into Katherine's eyes, still speaking. "Until you know you're safe!"

"Yes! How you reacted to Kami, Rachel, and I scared

us, and when you stopped coming out of your room and not talking with us! That really creeped us out!"

"You shouldn't have been looking through my window!"

"That's not the point! The point is that I'm really worried about you! You're taking Jon's death really hard and—"

"Don't speak his name, and don't bring him into this!"

"I'm gonna say his name and bring him into this! He was our friend too! And right now he's probably looking down at you from a better place thinking, hoping, that you come to your senses and realize that I need you! So do Rachel and Kami!"

"She's right, Zak. I'm really worried about you!" agreed Rachel. "And think about Kami and how she feels about you and ... and Brandon for Pete's sake! His *life* depends on you!"

"He tried to kill us! Why should I help him? He was probably the one who sent the Seekers that killed Jon!"

When Kami heard those words, she instantly became peeved and started screaming, "You know that wasn't him. Brandon would never do such a thing! Jon knew that! And you knew that, before this entire mess! It's not fair for you start saying things like that when you know they're not true!"

Zak shot up looking like a giant compared to everyone. They all backed up, pointing their guns at him, except for the three girls. "How do know for a fact that it really isn't him, huh?"

"Because I just know! That awful man probably made him do those things!"

"Whatever ... Just get out of here ... now!"

Katherine stepped closer to Zak. "No! Not until I get you better!"

Zak revealed a look of hate then reached for his blade. He pulled it out slowly. "Get out of this house now!" The cops continued to aim waiting for the order.

Rachel turned to the team knowing that if they shot, they wouldn't only make him mad, but they could possibly kill him. "Don't shoot, not unless he's close to killing someone!"

"No, I won't leave," replied Katherine, shaking her head. Zak swung his blade into the air and went to strike Katherine in half. Seeing this, Katherine jumped back and grabbed Rachel's spear, slamming on the button for the spear to come out on both sides. Zak looked up at Katherine and glided the blade to the left at her, one handed. Holding the spear in her right hand, Katherine blocked the attack. Kami grabbed her weapon out of her bag and helped Katherine, while Rachel stood there wondering why Katherine had to take *her* weapon.

Katherine and Kami were getting their behinds kicked; they had been cut on the sides, arms, and legs while Zak had nothing. Rachel continued to make sure that police stayed out of the way so that Katherine and Kami could handle the puppet. Zak shot his blade up from the bottom left up to the upper right then glided it across back to the left. Katherine pulled Kami back then down to dodge the strike. When she stood back up, Zak had his blade in the air, prepared to slice her in two. One thing stopped him though, and that was the fact that he had all the cops pointing their guns at him from all around.

"Put the blade away or we'll shoot!" warned a random cop.

"Fine, fine." Seeing the odds, Zak slipped the blade into the case hanging from his side.

"There." Zak grinned a fake grin, then backhanded Katherine across the face. She slid across the floor holding on to her cheek, sobbing. Zak's anger then dissolved, seeing and knowing what he just did made him come back to his senses. He clenched his fists and turned away in disgust with himself for not being strong enough to control his actions and anger. "K-Katherine, are you okay? I-I'm sorry."

"Zak, it's okay,"

"No it's not. Just...just get out."

"No!"

"Why?"

"Because I care about you way too much, and I'm not going to let you be in pain for the rest of your life." Rachel helped Katherine to her feet, and she walked toward Zak, wiping her tears away.

"I'm not mad, and I can tell that you held back and—"

He looked away and whispered, "That's not the point...I fought you then came back and hit you. No matter how hard...I still fought and hit you...I wasn't strong enough to control it..."

"I know you think that, but you *are* the strongest person I know, and..." She paused to catch her breath. "And you control yourself just fine. Jon's death caught you off guard, that's all. Now please...please look me in the eyes and say that to my face if you *truly* believe that." Tears poured down her cheeks as Zak looked up, slowly shaking his head.

Katherine lifted her hand and gently touched his cheek. "It's okay... It doesn't matter."

He then leaned toward her, lifting her chin up as she leaned toward him. "I'm sorry." he whispered before they pressed their lips softly up against one another.

⁂

Zak was finally recovering. Katherine led Zak outside and into the front lawn, where all the doctors were. They treated him, Katherine, and Kami.

⁂

A couple of days past, and Zak felt better than ever, but he didn't remember much of the experience, due to the different pills he had been taking. He did remember, though, Katherine and his kiss. He also remembered Jon's death, barely; he knew that he died but didn't really know how. All the other stuff with the experience remained a blur and may not ever come back. The three hoped it wouldn't, since they knew that it was a terrible memory to live with.

In the meantime of Zak's recovery, Kami packed up for the second part of the journey, the final part. On the final part, all that needed to be done was contact and ask Nick, the mayor of Brownten, and Bryan, the mayor of Wenstal, about them joining in the fight.

After about another month, the doctor said that Zak should be fine and that it was up to them if they wanted to tell him about what had happened on that day. The choice for that was... no. Zak packed up and loaded the luggage into a new truck that he bought, since the last one was completely destroyed by the enormous Seeker attack. At first Zak wondered where his truck was and what had happened to it, but the girls never told him so, being rich and all, he went out and bought a bigger and better one. Only two things were the same though and that was the color, gray, and the fact that the truck was a double door.

Once they were done with all the packing, Zak noticed that Katherine and Rachel hadn't packed anything or even prepared to go. It made him curious, and he soon asked about it. "Why aren't you guys preparing to go?"

"Because you... Oh, that's right!" exclaimed Rachel as she turned to Katherine and whispered to her. "Hey, we could go. Remember, he lost a lot of his memory; he doesn't remember ever telling us to stay home!"

"That's right!" Katherine then turned to Zak. "Hold on a sec, and we'll be out in a minute... okay?" Zak nodded and walked over to Kami as the other two sprinted into the house.

17

The trip wasn't as lively as it could have been since Jon passed away. The last words that he spoke, right before he died, started to jingle around in Kami's head when she suddenly and randomly said them aloud, "And give him a huge cheeseburger for me... also tell Zak that I'm going to miss him..."

Katherine, Rachel, and Zak looked at Kami with an awkward expression. "What?" asked Zak. Kami looked up and broke out of her daze.

"Oh, um... those were the last words Jon said... I don't know why, but they... just popped into my head."

"What's up with the cheeseburger?" questioned Rachel.

"I don't know. He wanted me to give one to Brandon if we were able to save him."

"Figures, even when he's dying, Jon always has to say something strange or stupid..." replied Rachel in a sarcastic tone.

Zak then looked back at Kami. "Did he really say that? About me?" Kami nodded and looked out the left window. Rachel was on the right, and Katherine sat up front with Zak.

This trip seemed to be taking longer than all the others; this was the sixth day on the road.

The land was huge, almost half of the earth, and all together in one huge clump with the exceptions of lakes and rivers. It was named Savania. There were smaller islands around Savania, like the ones by Wenstal such as Stravage Island, Carina, and Banner Village. Another good-sized piece of land on the other side of the earth was called Fredrena. In between the two great lands, on each side, were smaller, but still big landmasses. The one on the right, at the view from Savania was known as Nelmena, and the one on the left was Kili Islands surrounded each of the masses.

On the seventh day, at around midnight, they finally reached Brownten. The city didn't look that much different from the last time. Things still looked like they died.

Before heading over to the city hall, Zak decided to stay the night at a hotel and have a fresh start in the morning.

They pulled into a front spot, since the parking lot was barely filled and unpacked their belongings.

After they checked in, reached the room, and settled in, they decided that each person would get their own room.

Once in the door, they had to walk through an entryway in order to get into the living room. Walking through the entryway, the kitchen opened to the left. The living room was spacious, and in the middle of the left wall there was a thirty-six-inch TV sitting upon a stand; on the right wall, in the middle was an opening leading into a mini hallway. Connecting to the hallway were the four rooms, two on each side. The front right room was

Rachel's, and the far right was Kami's. Then on the front left was Katherine's and the far left was Zak's.

Before they went to bed, Zak sat on the couch watching TV with Katherine next to him. His arm was placed across her shoulders as they watched a stupid night show, as for Rachel and Kami, they observed from Rachel's room at an angle so they could get a front row view. The door had a small crack, so only one person could look at a time; the crack was hard to see so Katherine never seemed to notice.

The show wasn't really entertaining, but it was still funny for Kami and Rachel, knowing that they were watching without Katherine or Zak knowing. It always seemed like they had eyes in the back of their heads and knew all of their movements.

After a low laugh, Kami calmed herself and asked, "What do you think they would do if they found out that we were watching?"

"I don't know. But that's why we make sure they never do..." Rachel stopped for a second and looked through the crack, making sure they didn't see. She saw Katherine stand up, Zak following; they walked toward the mini hallway by the room. Her heart started to pump faster and faster, scared that they *really did* notice but didn't do anything, until now.

They walked closer and closer until they stopped in the middle between Katherine's and Rachel's rooms. They mumbled words to each other as Rachel made the crack smaller praying to God that the two wouldn't find out. The two lovebirds kissed each other good night and slipped into their rooms. Rachel backed away, fully closing the door behind her, announcing what she just saw to

Kami as she took deep breaths in and out. "Well, that was nerve racking... But don't worry, you didn't really miss anything. All they did kiss each other good night and go to their rooms."

"Okay... well, I better be getting in bed." Kami stood up and tiptoed out the door and into her room as Rachel went into the bathroom. They changed into their pajamas and went to sleep.

※

"Ha! Your crazy plan didn't work, and Zak's better than ever!" bragged Brandon in a low, yet happy tone as he chuckled in pain. Kevin spun around quickly and slapped Brandon across the face, and a loud echo followed for seven seconds. Brandon's head flung to the right and bobbled back to its original spot. A huge, deep red mark was left on Brandon's face, but instead of yelping in pain, Brandon laughed. Kevin turned around facing the opposite way of Brandon and started to mumble to himself. Brandon looked up at him and tried to make out the gibberish. "What... how is... they... with the police... when should... Seekers... where though?"

Kevin walked slowly out of the room and continued to talk to himself. Once he was out, a Seeker walked in holding a ring of keys. Brandon was let out of the chains holding him to the wall and dragged out of the room. He shut his eyes and tried to hope for the best.

Before Brandon reopened his eyes, he felt the cold water on the bottom of his worn-out feet. A chill jogged up and down Brandon's spine; he knew what was going to happen to him. The room he was in was the drowning room. He'd been in here at least five different times, times that were horrible. The Seeker threw Brandon to the ground and forced him to kneel before something; he opened his eyes to see in front of him a wide pool of water. A light above him shone brightly, giving Brandon a headache as he squinted.

Ahead of him, behind the water was nothing but pure darkness. When Brandon heard a door slam within the black, he knew that he was going to be interrogated. He thought to himself, *if I say the wrong thing, I'm going to be dunked, and if I say the truth about what I think is going to happen, I'm going to endanger them.*

A voice then came up behind Brandon and asked, "What have you heard Kami and the others say about getting into this place?"

"I-I don't know," replied Brandon fearfully.

"That's a lie!" screamed the voice as a hand pushed Brandon's head down into the pool unexpectedly. What was one minute seemed to be like ten years. Brandon tried to hold his breath, but all the air was escaping away from him, and his life soon began to flash before his eyes.

Normally Brandon could hold his breath for a while, but when dunked suddenly caught off guard and not being able to take in a breath of air, holding his breath was a lot more difficult.

Finally Brandon was pulled back up into the sweet oxygen. Water slid off his face as he breathed hard and heavy. Brandon loosened his muscles and leaned to the left. Kevin grabbed the wet mop, Brandon's hair, and yanked it back, forcing Brandon to look up into the blinding light. "Now tell me what route you've heard them talking about!"

Brandon coughed and answered. "I-I don't-don't know!" Kevin shoved Brandon's head into the water and pulled it back up then dunked him again. This time when he pulled Brandon back up, Kevin grabbed Brandon's hair and pulled him up by that.

Yelping in terrible pain, Brandon knew in his mind that he would never speak of the correct route that Kami would take.

"Fine, don't answer... I'll make sure they never have the chance stop my plans... with or without your useless information!" Kevin reached into his pockets and pulled out a pair of bracelets and forced them onto Brandon's wrists. Brandon started to doze off, but when the mad man pressed a button on the remote he held in his hands, a blue beam shot out of a hole in one of the bracelets, wrapped around his wrists. The beam sliced through a little of Brandon's flesh and started getting hotter and hotter. Kevin walked out of the room, leaving Brandon scrambling to pull the bracelets off.

The moon set and the sun rose to reveal a bright and beautiful day. Instead of a nice slow wake up, a bucket of ice-cold water was tossed onto Kami. Kami jumped and screamed as the cold water fell against her thin blanket and seeped onto her. She sat up on the bed, wide awake now, to see that the ones who caused the unpleasant wake up were Katherine and Zak.

Katherine knelt down and whispered to Kami in a fun tone. "Gotcha back for spying."

Kami tilted her head to the right, then remembered

last night and laughed, still shivering. "H-how d-did y-you know?"

"How could we have not known, you guys were laughing *really* loud!" answered Zak when Rachel came running into the room dripping water on the ground.

"So th-they g-got you t-too?"

Kami removed the thin wet blanket off her freezing body and replied, "Y-yea. N-now if y-you w-will pl-please e-excuse me, I'm g-getting in the sh-shower!" As Kami wobbled over to the bathroom door, Katherine and Zak started to cracking up laughing, and Rachel left the room.

Once Kami was out of the shower and dressed, she packed all of her things back into her suitcase and walked out into the living room. She set her bag down on the couch and saw Rachel in the kitchen making blueberry, chocolate chip pancakes.

"Ooh, those look really good."

"After I finally regained all my body heat and changed, I had a craving for them and decided to make some before we left,"

"That's awesome... When will they be ready?"

"In just like, two minutes... Hey, go ask Zak when we're leaving."

"Okay, where is he?"

"I think he's in his room, but I'm not quite sure,"

"Okay." Kami walked off into the mini hallway and knocked on Zak's door. She waited a sec, but there was no reply, she figured that he must have gotten in the shower or something so she walked back into the living room. "He's probably in the shower, because there was no reply."

"No? He just stepped out like ten minutes ago,"

"Okay, well, I'll check out on the balcony." Kami started toward the sliding glass door at the back of the room.

She cracked the door and saw Zak leaning on the railing looking at the old pond across the street. Kami stepped out and asked, "Hey, Rachel wants to know what time we're leaving."

Zak turned his head and answered, "Oh, um, well in about ten, fifteen minutes."

"Okay." Kami felt something odd with Zak and started to ask him if he was okay. "Hey, Zak, are you okay 'cause you seem sad?"

Zak turned around. "Nah, I'm fine, just thinking about what to say to Nick when we get over to the city hall."

※-※

After breakfast, Zak loaded the luggage back into the truck, and they all piled in. The city hall wasn't far away, so it wasn't a bad drive at all. They pulled into a parking space and jumped out eager to hear Nick's answer. The four climbed the steps in the front and walked around the several halls and corners until they reached Nick's office. Zak walked in relatively quick as the others followed.

"Zak? Why are you back? Not that it's a bad thing, but it is unexpected," questioned Nick as he stood up from his desk and walked over toward Zak.

"Well, I came to ask you a very important question, and I need an answer right away, if you could," replied Zak.

"Yea, sure. What?"

"Well, you remember how last time I came I asked you if you had seen that friend of Kami's, but you said that you hadn't?"

"Yes."

"Well, that guy needs your help."

"Mine?"

"Yes, you see, we have a theory that has a pretty big chance of being correct, and that is that he is being held captive by Kevin Beraldi."

"Kevin Beraldi!?"

"Yea, we have reason to believe that he escaped and went after Brandon, the guy who needs your help, for revenge against his father."

"Wait, this Brandon guy, you think that his father was George?"

"Yes, and we believe that somehow he's controlling Brandon in doing all these things that he would never do."

"Okay... so what do you need me for?"

"We need you to prepare an army to help invade, or provide a distraction, so that we can get into the old mansion he has."

"How do you know that he's in the mansion?"

"We don't know for a fact, but it's a theory presented from the past."

"Hmm, I don't know. How many soldiers would you need? And have you asked any of the other mayors?"

"Yes, we have asked others, and it doesn't matter on how many soldiers."

"Well..."

"After we're done here, we are going to ask Bryan."

"Oh, Bryan, huh. Well, you can count me in. I'll have around one hundred soldiers ready."

"Thanks, Nick."

"Yea, don't mention it."

Zak turned around and started to walk out of the room when he heard a girl scream from outside of the city hall. Nick, Zak, Katherine, Rachel, and Kami all ran outside as fast as they could.

18

Brandon stood at the foot of the stairs of city hall, holding a young six-year-old girl captive. He had his blade positioned up against her neck, ready to strike at any moment. "We meet again, but it seems that one of your group is missing?" No one said anything so Brandon broke the silence. "So no one's talking. Well okay then. I guess that this girl isn't that important to this society." Brandon raised his blade and went to strike, but instead of hitting the girl, he hit the blade that Zak had launched at him. Brandon balanced himself, and Zak stepped forward.

"We know what's wrong with you, and we're here to help. So let us help you figure out how Kevin is controlling you and we'll fight it together."

Brandon burst out laughing, wiping tears from his eyes; when he stopped, he looked up at Zak, who had a face of stone. "Oh, wow, you were serious! That's even better! I'm not being 'controlled.' I'm me and no one else, so back off that subject!"

"Let the girl go!"

"Why? She's the only thing that is allowing us to

spend this quality time together, to better understand each other and our motives!"

"Leave her out of this; we're just trying to help you!"

"I don't need help. I never have!"

"You know that's not true!" Zak stepped again, but Brandon went for the girl, who was trembling in fear. Tears ran down the little girl's cheeks, her face turned red, and she clutched the doll in her hands tighter and tighter.

"Where's the little girl's mother?!" cried out Zak as Brandon glared at him.

"Her mother's gone."

"What do you mean 'gone'? Is she dead?"

"No, she's gone. She lost track of the girl, and that's when I snatched her!"

"What kind of sick person are you?!"

"Me? Sick? How can you say that after sulking in your room for days without—"

Suddenly a dagger stabbed Brandon in the arm. He laughed for a second then spoke. "Wow, this is great. He lost his memory, and you guys didn't tell him about what happened, so when I almost did, you had to find a way to shut me up. Well, I give it a clap or two, but you still have much to learn." He pulled the dagger out of his flesh and threw it to the ground beside him and held his arm where the dagger was. The child beside him sat too scared to move, just holding her doll as tightly as possible.

Once he let go, after a few seconds, the wound was gone. Everyone's jaw dropped at how he did the magic trick. "How, how did you do that?" asked Kami, stepping closer to get a better look.

Brandon looked up and pretended to dust his arm off. "What?"

"How did you... Where's the cut?"

"Oh, it doesn't matter! That's one of the things that you need to find out for yourself." Brandon resumed his position, holding the little girl hostage.

"What do you want in exchange for the girl?!" demanded Nick.

"It's very simple, really. All I want is Kami, and *I* will never ever come to this city or any others ever again."

"How do we know that you're not lying?!"

"Well, I guess that you're just gonna to have to believe that I'm telling the truth."

Zak turned to Nick and whispered to him, "The only thing that he's wanted the entire time is Kami, but we don't know what he's going to do to her."

"Have a decision in ten minutes or else this city will end up being just like Lenowa!" Then and there, Brandon vanished into thin air without a trace. The little girl, still frightened, stood up and looked around, wondering where her captor went. Katherine and Rachel rushed over to the girl and comforted her, picking up their weapons, while Nick, Zak, and Kami talked about what had just happened.

"What happened to Lenowa?" asked Nick.

"The whole city was destroyed, and all the people living there were killed, piled in the park, and burned," answered Kami sadly.

"After that a huge army of Seekers, like thousands of them, attacked us. But what I'd like to know is what was he talking about in the beginning with all the sulking," finished Zak.

Kami looked at him. "It was nothing; he just made things up to entertain himself."

Nick looked around at the city he was mayor of. "I know it doesn't look grand and magnificent like Broad City, but it's still the home of many and to me. I can't have this Brandon guy just destroy it, and though it pains me to say, we have to give Kami to him."

"I know, but we don't know what's going to happen to her if we do," replied Zak uncomfortably.

"Is there a way for you to contact Wenstal, in the next four minutes?" questioned Kami.

"Well, I guess we could use the super computer. Why?"

"We weren't able to contact anyone because our computer was busted, so if you could contact Wenstal, get Bryan to agree to helping us in trying to get inside the mansion, then maybe if I go with Brandon, and you guys just be there soon, then maybe you all can get me out of there and save Brandon without having the city destroyed!"

"I guess it wouldn't hurt to try," Nick replied as he ran back into the building.

Once inside the computer room, Nick sat on a chair and looked for the way to contact Wenstal. Kami and Zak were in the room talking about what would happen when the time came for her to go with Brandon, while Katherine and Rachel took the little girl home. "Wait, do you remember what happened last time we tried to do something like this?" pondered Kami.

Zak looked at her. "Yes, oh man, Seekers could have been outside listening to all that we were saying!"

"I know. What are we going to do now?"

"I don't know. That seems to be the only plan that actually had a chance of working out. But before we go into that, we need to inspect the room." Zak and Kami started to look around and check all the objects in the room; it didn't take that long since the room didn't have much in it.

"So if the plan we discussed outside works, then that's awesome, but what are we going to do if it doesn't work?" asked Kami.

"I don't think that we should do the original plan," replied Zak.

Concerned Kami tilted her head and asked, "Why?"

"Because why even try when there's a good chance Brandon had Seekers listening and waste the lives of many?"

"You have a point there... Then what are we going to do?" Nick turned around, looking at Zak. "I've contacted Bryan; he's in. I've also contacted Broad City and told both cities to start heading for Andren, so what's the plan?"

"I don't know; Seekers could have easily been spying on us, so I don't think that we should use that plan."

"That's understandable."

"I'm still going with Brandon, no matter what. I'm not going to allow him to harm innocent people," interrupted Kami.

"I don't know if you are," argued Zak.

"I am, and there's nothing you can do to stop me. And besides, I know that you're going to find a way to get me out of there along with Brandon."

"Don't be too sure of that."

"I know you will, okay, and I have faith in you and God. He'll help you find a way."

Zak grinned for a sec then started to think about another option.

"Come on, Zak, trust me. I can take care of myself,"

"Zak, I say she's right. She really has no choice but to go. We don't have really any other options," Nick announced. "I know but... All right; fine," caved in Zak still insecure. "Kami, I'm going to give you this chip, okay? It's going to be placed in your ear; it won't go in too far but far enough that no one will see. What it will do is it will allow me to hear everything that is being said—what you say and what anyone else says through this computer," explained Nick as Katherine and Rachel walked in.

"So how are things in here going?" asked Rachel. Zak turned around.

"Fine, just fine. She's going with Brandon," he said in a little angry sarcastic tone.

"Really?" both girls asked, and Zak nodded his head. They both looked shocked at the idea, but with Zak saying yes, it made it a double shock.

"Are you sure that it's a good idea?" Katherine asked.

"I don't think it is, but she does, and there's no stopping her when she says that she's *going* to do something," answered Zak, and all three of them turned to Kami, who was getting help putting the chip in the right way by Nick.

Once she was done with that, Kami walked toward the others. "Okay, I'm ready. How much time to we have?"

"About a minute," Zak said uncomfortably.

"Okay, well, we better get out there! He'll be here soon, and if we're not out there, he might think that we left and destroy the city!" exclaimed Kami as if everyone was okay with what she was doing.

They stepped outside at exactly the right time; Brandon appeared in front of them, dressed in all black—a tight black T-shirt that showed off his muscles and black skinny jeans with black shoes.

"Have you made your decision yet?" he asked.

"Yes, we have," Zak said a little angry.

"Good, good, so what is it? Hand over Kami or have this entire city obliterated." Brandon smiled as he awaited an answer.

Just then Kami stepped forward. "You're taking me!"

"Oh? Really? Wow, okay then." Brandon stretched his hand forward, signaling her to come to him. Slowly walking to him, Kami's heartbeat sped up. Though she was confident in her decision and in Zak, Rachel, and Katherine, she couldn't help be scared for what lay ahead. Kami lifted her hand up and placed it on Brandon's very gracefully. He gripped her hand and grinned, jerking her to his side, and they both vanished in seconds.

19

Kami was gone. There was no way to get her back unless they joined forces with everyone. Zak, Katherine, and Rachel leaped into the truck after the incident and took off for Andren. At this point, Zak didn't care what it took, he was going to get back to Andren as fast as possible; he wasn't going to lose another person he cared deeply about, and after hearing what Kami had seen with Brandon, he wasn't going to let that happen to her either.

On the way back to Andren, Zak was excessively speeding. This was fine since no one, including the cops *ever* left the cities. But when they entered Andren, problems started to happen. First, since Zak wasn't thinking, he was pulled over for excessive speeding, was caught in five o'clock traffic, and when they reached the house, the computer wouldn't work. When it finally did, the computer took forever to boot; once the computer fully booted, the connections to communication failed, so Zak had to fix that. And after an hour of tinkering with the thing, Zak fixed the communications, but the mayor of Andren wouldn't answer her call.

So Zak, Rachel, and Katherine had to jump back into the truck and ride across the city to get to the city hall. Sprinting through the halls and bursting through the door, they were finally able to talk to Lindsey, the mayor of Andren. Zak started to talk, still heavily breathing.

"Lindsey, we...need your...help right...away, and...I...can't take no...for an answer!"

Lindsey, still shocked from the door being kicked open, tried to speak. "Um, o-okay? What do you need?"

"I need you to gather an army, fast! We have reason to believe that Kevin Beraldi has escaped from his prison!"

"What!"

"Yes, and we also believe that he's holding a guy by the name of Brandon captive and using him to take down anyone and everyone that gets in the way of his plans. When we were in Brownten, he forced us to give him our friend Kami or else he would send Brownten into oblivion! Just like he did Lenowa!"

"What! This is terrible! Have you contacted everyone?"

"Yes. We need to hurry. I don't want Kami to be tortured like Brandon!"

"This Brandon guy is being tortured?!"

"Well, it's a long story, but we have reason to believe that. Now hurry; all the other cities will be here in about an hour. They all know that this is an emergency, so they're coming fast!"

"Okay, okay." Lindsey stood up and jogged for the door with all the others following.

On the way to the computer room, Lindsey turned around. "So Lenowa has been destroyed, huh? Well, did anyone make it?"

Zak looked at her with disappointment and shook his head. "No, everyone was killed and burned." Lindsey didn't say anything more, she just looked ahead.

When they entered in the computer room, they all helped in checking the room to make sure that there were no Seekers, and it was a good thing too, because they found three of them, one as a mouse hooked up to the super computer, another as a desk off to the side and the last as a pencil on the floor. Lindsey had Zak get on the computer to tell the general of the army of Andren about what had happened. They were on a Web cam.

"General, we need the army now! There is no other way to get into the mansion!" exclaimed Zak.

The general replied, "How do you know that he's in the mansion?"

"I don't know for sure, but that's the only place that he's ever been to, so that's where we need to start. And I know for a fact that he's not in any of the cities. As for the villages, I have no idea."

"Okay, fine. I'll gather a force and meet you and the others in front of the mansion at seven o'clock."

"Thank you. But, general, I won't be there. I'll be heading through the back. The reason why I need you and the others is because I need a distraction."

"Okay, so do all the others know that?"

"No, not really. That's why I need you to be in charge of the entire thing."

"Okay, then you be careful!"

"Understood, and the same to you." Zak reached forward and stopped the camera then disconnected it. He turned around to look at Katherine. "All right, I want you and Rachel to help in the distraction. I'm going in through the back alone."

"Why? She's our friend too!"

"Please, Katherine, stay in the front where it's safe! I can't lose another person I care about!"

"Neither can I! That's why I want to come with you! I don't want to be in the front wondering if your still alive or not!"

"Please, Zak?" pleaded Rachel.

Zak thought for a moment then answered, "No! And that's final; I'm going in alone!"

Katherine shook her head in disbelief. "I know you think that you're going to have to protect me, but you're wrong!"

"That's not true. I just can't lose you or Rachel or Kami like I lost Jon. I may not remember how he died, but I know that he's gone, and that can't happen to you guys!"

"I understand. I'll do whatever I can to help..." said Katherine. Rachel nodded in agreement. Zak led them out of the room with Lindsey following.

※ ※

"Yes, my plan is coming together, finally!"

"Where is Brandon!?"

"You don't need to know, all you need to know is that your friends will fail in their attempts to rescue you!"

"No, they won't, and you can go die for all I care!" Kevin smacked Kami across the face and left the room, but as he did a Seeker came in holding something under its arm. It seemed to be dripping water everywhere, and it didn't look like it was alive. Its legs and arms drooped down hanging as if they were four pieces of string. The Seeker tossed it across the room and left. The thing didn't budge. Kami, still chained to the blood-stained wall, called out, "Brandon? Brandon, is that you?" The object didn't move, but it started to groan softly. With the moan Kami knew that it *was* Brandon.

He looked even more beaten than last time, his hair had grown out, and he had lost a lot more weight. He had whip marks and scars from the whip and claws that stretched across from his back to his ribs. He was drenched in water and had burns on his neck, arms, and feet.

After a minute or two of silence, Brandon finally started to move, slowly but surely. He rolled over to his other side, so that he could see Kami. "Why…why are…are you…here?"

"I'm here because I wanted to help you!"

"No…no…you…should have…never…come!" He tried to speak, but it came out quiet and a little slurred.

"Why? Don't you want to be rescued?"

"You're not…rescuing…me…he's going….to…make me…kill…you."

"What!" Just as Kami finished saying what she did, she noticed something very odd. She noticed that the deep cut the dagger made back at Brownten was still there. Kami stared at it for a minute, trying figure out how the cut could heal so fast then just reappear in the exact same spot. "Hey, um, Brandon, how did you get that cut on your arm?"

Brandon looked at it and replied, "You should know; you were there."

"Then how did you heal?"

"There's a—." Just as he was about to say, Kevin came in.

"So, Kami, I want you to tell me everything that you know about the attempts to get into this mansion!"

She gave him an evil glare and started, "And if I don't?"

"Well, ask Brandon what happens. He's been through it numerous times. He wouldn't cooperate and tell me all the knowledge he contained, so I had to get it out somehow."

Brandon looked up and tried to see out of the black eye he had.

"All right we're in front of the mansion, waiting for orders," spoke the general.

Zak picked up his walkie-talkie and pressed on the talk button. "Okay, are Rachel and Katherine there with you?"

"Yes, sir."

"Okay, good. I'm on the cliff right now, so proceed in attacking the front."

"Understood." Zak slipped the walkie-talkie into the case attached to his belt. He stretched his arm to grab onto a piece of rock and stuck his foot onto the ledge his hand was just on.

Meanwhile, out front, the starting forces ran into the mansion. Things seemed quiet, too quiet. The soldiers walked around, guns close to them, cocked. Nothing seemed out of the ordinary, just a normal old mansion.

Zak was getting closer and closer to the mansion

when he heard his walkie-talkie ring. He picked it up and pressed on the talk button. "Yea?"

"Zak, there's nothing in this mansion; just the same since the last time I was in here after the whole mess. We've checked everywhere!"

"Well...just keep checking, I'm just about to the top, just a few more feet."

"Okay, but I doubt...ugh." The walkie-talkie suddenly went dead, making the fuzzy noise.

Zak tried over and over to get it back on. "General? General? General, come in! Ugh, this thing is useless!" Zak threw the walkie-talkie into the water below and continued to climb, except faster, worried that all the people had been killed by hidden Seekers, even Rachel and Katherine.

The second Zak reached the top; he ripped off all the gear he needed to climb the mountain and ran into the mansion. Pulling out his blade, Zak feared for the worst and ran as fast as he could. Until he came across Katherine standing in front of him. She looked like a zombie, from the way she stood and how her head tilted to the side, dead like. He stopped and examined her for a sec. "Katherine? Where is the general?" She didn't answer, so he looked into her eyes. Seeing nothing, he raised his blade and went to charge at it, but as he did the Seeker screamed a loud screeching scream. Zak stopped and plugged his ears. When he looked up, the Seeker disappeared.

※ ※

"You see, now that I have the power to control these wonderful beings known as Seekers, I get anything and everything I want! And what I want is revenge, sweet revenge!"

"How is this revenge? You're attacking the perpetrator's son! Not the actual perpetrator!"

Kevin dunked Kami then brought her back up by the hair. "I didn't get the sweet, wonderful feeling of revenge when the Seekers killed his dad, and I wanted that feeling more than anything, so I'm using the next best thing, his son."

"What does this have to do with me?"

"This plan has everything to do with you! When you get hurt or Brandon feels that you're in pain, it tears him up inside. Oh and by the way, he's been watching you on this quest the entire time, due to my Seekers of course, but he has done everything in his power to help you and the others, and you know what I do? I crush what he tries to do!"

"You sick freak!"

Kevin slapped her then dunked her. When she was brought back up, he continued. "Anyway, I bet you think that we're in Andren, don't you?"

"Yea, why?"

"You're just like Zak; you think that after two different tries to get revenge and have those plans spoiled that I would go back to the same place that the cops know by heart?!"

"Well…"

"I'm not stupid!" Kevin signaled for a Seeker, and he left the room.

Zak reached the grand hall and saw no one, then remembered the secret passage that connected to the lab that Kevin stayed in last time.

Zak used to sneak off during school and play in the house, after the first incident, and discovered that a vase in one of the halls, when pulled down, opened up into a secret passage and when he went down the stairs he would encounter a lab. Zak ran through the entire house pulling all the vases that he could find, but when he ended up in the dining room, which was huge, he saw a mini army of Seekers in front of him. "So that's what the screech did. No problem; this ought to be fun," whispered Zak to himself cockily as he cracked a grin. The Seekers started to sprint toward him; in response, Zak raised his blade.

One by one, Zak took out any Seeker around him. One Seeker started to grow its nails out, but Zak jumped into the air and stabbed it in the head. Another tried to come from behind, so Zak tucked the blade under his arm and jammed it into the Seeker. Four others leaped into the air; as Zak faced others, the four had their nails fully grown out and sliced down Zak's back. Ignoring the serious pain, Zak swung his blade around killing the last of the Seekers. He rubbed his hand on his back to feel how the cuts were, and when he did, a shock of pain hit him in the spine. The blood was worse than the actual cut, so Zak kept moving.

When he finally found the correct vase, he walked down the stairwell to find that the lab was empty. He looked around a little more and saw a big black door next to an operation table. On the table he saw a big green button.

He headed toward the black door, walking slowly and unsure; he cautiously opened it. Inside he felt a cold breeze hit him. The entire room was made of blue bricks. He found blood everywhere and one little window at the top let barely any light in. Over in one of the corners, he saw dried vomit and waste. A pole sat in the room, covered in blood. Two leather bonds, for the wrists to go through, were on the sides. A bowl half full of ketesh lay in the middle of the room. Zak looked in it and saw the ketesh, almost throwing up himself, from the smell and looks.

Was this what Brandon went through? Zak continued through the room, on the wall he saw two chains sticking out, each one had a metal wristband connected to the end of the chain. The wall was blood stained. The place filled Zak with sorrow as he pictured Kevin torturing Brandon. He felt as if he heard the cries Brandon yelled out. Zak ran to the exit and closed the door behind him hoping, more than ever, to get Brandon out of the clutches of Kevin.

Zak continued to examine the lab; he saw another door that was navy blue. Zak headed for it and opened it slowly; inside he found a spotlight shining down on a wide pool of water. *How sick was this man? Would he drown Brandon? Would he?* Zak saw that there was nothing else in the room, so he walked out and looked at the desk in the corner and in all the file cabinets.

As he did that, another door caught his eye, a red one. Zak walked in and saw a furnace, with a branding iron heating up. Zak picked the iron up and saw that there was no brand just a flat hot surface. Looking up, Zak saw a table next to the furnace, on the sides were wristbands that Brandon's hands had gone through. *He would even burn him?*

After searching the entire place, Zak looked at the operation table he passed on the way to the black door. All these odd lights were blinking and switches were turned on or off, but one button stood out, and that was the huge green button. At the bottom of the button there was a black print reading, *Teleportation. Select destination using keyboard.* Zak looked around for the keyboard, and then felt that it was underneath the table. He pulled it out, but as he did he heard cries coming from all around.

Zak stopped and looked at the room; no one else was in the room beside him. The cries continued. Zak stepped forward and called out, "Is anyone there?"

"Yes. Zak? Zak, is that you?" a voice shouted. It sounded faded, but Zak yelled out again.

"Keep talking, I'm following your voice!"

"Zak, please help. We're in a chamber in the lab." Zak laid his hands on the bricks hoping that one of them opened another secret passage.

The voice went on, and Zak finally found the switch, it was one of the file cabinets. Zak heard the voice coming from behind a file cabinet, so when he went to move it the wall came out and moved to the right. All the soldiers came rushing out. It was about four hundred, and then Rachel and Katherine came out. When the room was empty, it revealed a gigantic open space.

Katherine came out running to Zak; her arms were open as Zak grabbed her and held on without letting go. She looked up at him and started to cry while shaking her head. "Oh my gosh, we...we saw Kevin take Kami, and behind them a...a Seeker was...was dragging Brandon...and he looked so horrible...so much blood...and groaning and..." Zak put his hands on

Katherine's head, and she dug her head into his chest and cried. Rachel stood in front of them crying into her hands when a man all dressed in camouflage walked up to her. Rachel noticed his nametag said Ryan. Everyone saw Brandon and what Kevin had done to him.

※※

"Brandon! Brandon! Stop it! Leave him alone!" cried Kami, as she witnessed Brandon being whipped on the pole.

"Kami! Ugh..." Brandon tightened his muscles trying not to show pain for Kami. "Don't—ah—don't worry about... me!"

"Kevin, stop! Please!" She urged herself forward trying with all her might to get free "Kevin! Stop!" Kami's attempts to get to Brandon failed, and she was forced to watch Brandon get beaten, knowing that there was nothing that she could do to help him.

※※

"We need to help Brandon, no matter what it takes! We took all the things that we knew about him for granted, and look at what he's been through, when it wasn't even his fault!" exclaimed Katherine with determination. Zak thought for a second about where else he would go.

Then suddenly the answer popped into his head. "That's it. Kevin has both Kami and Brandon, right? Yes, and what do they have in common?"

Rachel and Katherine thought for a moment then shouted, "They both came from the same village!"

"Correct, but do you guys know what village?"

No one answered; Zak didn't even know.

The general then stepped up and created a solution to the problem. "Do you have some of her DNA?"

Rachel thought back to the things that she let Kami borrow and remembered that she had let Kami borrow a pair of her pajamas. "I think that I might have some! Just stay here, and I'll take the truck and be right back."

Rachel started up the stairs, and Katherine called out, "I'm coming too!" and she ran after Rachel.

20

"Yes, her DNA is here. Now all we have to do is trace it back to her profile from the super computer in the city hall. Since Andren is the main city of Savania, it should come up," stated the general.

"But didn't the villagers refuse to be in the computer?" asked Rachel.

"Yes, but she may have family in the cities. All we'd have to do it is call that family and ask what village she's from!"

"Why do we need her DNA?"

"We need it because our system was backed up, and the automatic ways for everything are down, so we have to do everything manually, almost."

"Oh, okay, sorry, I'm not a big techno person. That's why I have Zak!" joked Rachel.

"Okay, we have her! She has an older sister who lives in Broad City. The number is…"

"Okay, I have her," announced Katherine. "Hello? Oh hi, my name is Katherine Kiraly, and I'm a friend of Kami's."

"Oh, hello. I'm Kami's older sister. What can I help you with?"

"Well, I'm working with the military at the moment, and if you could tell me what village Kami lived in, that would be awesome!"

"Why do you need to know?"

"Kami is in danger. She's been taken prisoner by Kevin Beraldi. Yes, he did escape. We have confirmed that, and we need this information so that we can get to her and save her!"

"Oh my gosh! Kevin Beraldi! Um…" The woman went on with shock. "Okay, she lived in…"

"Ma'am, if you could please hurry that would be great!"

"Sorry, okay, I have it. She lived in Banner Village."

"Okay, thank you so much."

"Please help my little sister!"

"We are doing our best." Katherine hung up her cell phone. "We're going to Banner Village!"

❧-❦

Even with the military pass, it still took four days to get to the village. It was small but peaceful, friendly, and beautiful. The four hundred soldiers turned into Katherine, Rachel, Zak, the general, and twenty other men, including Ryan. They all asked around, amongst the villagers. No one seemed to remember Kami or Brandon, but one particular couple did.

"Excuse me, ma'am. Do you by chance know who Kami is? Or Brandon?" asked Ryan. The woman's eyes widened, and she took in a great breath.

"Oh my gosh, my Kami! My sweet baby! Have you seen her? Oh, where is she? I've missed her so much! I lost her so long ago!"

"Ma'am we *have* seen her, but a man by the name of Kevin Beraldi has taken her captive along with a guy named Brandon."

"Brandon!? Oh, Brandon was her best friend! He was always such a cute sweetheart! What has happened to them? Where are they? And who is this Kevin Beraldi?"

Ryan looked over his shoulder and called for Zak. "Here's one who knows who they are!" Ryan then turned back to the woman. "Ma'am, can I please have your name?"

"Oh yes, it's Margaret Shalown,"

"Thank you. Now please wait here for our friend Zak." Ryan walked toward Zak, and Zak walked up to her.

"Margaret Shalown? My name is Zak Delltoria. Kami was a friend of mine and I'm trying to find her and Brandon. Do you have any idea where they might be?"

"No, I don't; I'm sorry. I haven't seen those two in forever!"

"Okay thank you for your time."

"Oh but my husband might have. You see, I'm her mother and my husband is her father. He works in the fields in the back."

"Okay, well, I need to go..." Zak pulled his blade out and jammed it into the woman in front of him; as he did, he whispered to her, "Just because you talk doesn't mean you have a soul."

All the others came running up as villagers started to circle around Zak. "Zak, are you sure that was a Seeker?" asked Rachel.

"Yes. Like I've said before, the eyes are everything. I hadn't ever come across a Seeker that could talk... until now."

"We're sorry for disturbing your daily routines. Please ignore us!" announced the general to the crowds that started to form.

"You killed her!" shouted one of the villagers.

"No, no, that wasn't Margaret. Now please go back to what you were doing!" Zak pulled his blade out from the Seeker and backed up from it so that the crowd could see that it wasn't a real person. The body switched from the woman to the Seeker.

The crowd screamed and backed away. "What is that?!" cried one of the villagers.

"What happened?!" screamed another.

"How did that happen?!" yelled another when Zak started to speak. "Everyone, give me your attention; give me your attention!" All the panic and chaos slowed down and eventually stopped. "I know that all this is new to you! That was a Seeker! I need your help. A friend of mine was captured by the person who is controlling the Seekers, so if you have any idea where a guy named Kevin Beraldi is, then please let me know! This is *extremely* important!"

At that moment, a younger boy stepped forward, a little nervous. "I think I know where Kami is!"

Zak shoved everyone out of his way to reach the boy. "Hi, my name is Zak. Please tell me what you know about Kami and Brandon!"

"Um, I saw a man and a dark green thing like the one you just killed carrying a girl and dragging a beaten animal through the woods when I was getting wood for the house. I saw it this morning, and I think that they headed for the house on the small island. Do you want me to show you the island?"

Zak looked surprised at the knowledge the boy contained then replied, "Yes, yes that would be awesome!"

"Okay, then come on," The boy started to run through the village with Zak, the general, Katherine, Rachel, Ryan, and the other nineteen men following.

They had run through the entire forest to come to a cliff. Across from them, they saw a small lone island or cliff, with one good-sized house sitting upon it. The island didn't seem to have rocks around, so they would have to swim across and climb up. On that cliff was their best bet. Zak looked at the boy and asked, "What's your name?"

"Santos."

"Well, Santos, I thank you so much for telling us about what you saw." As Zak continued, he looked deeply into the teen's eyes; he saw a soul. "You could have saved two lives today."

"Thank you for coming out here from the city to save these two people." The teen smiled.

Zak tilted his head in confusion. "How did you know that we came from the city?"

"Well, people around here don't dress like you, and we don't stab fellow villagers."

Zak chuckled a little then smiled. "Yea, I guess those gave it away, and once again thanks for the help."

"Sure thing." The teen turned around and started to run back to the village.

"You're good with kids, did you know that?" pointed out Katherine.

"No, I'm really not. Normally I scare them."

They all laughed, then Katherine came back and said, "No, really you are."

"Okay, whatever you say," joked Zak as he grabbed some of his gear and put it on. "I need you guys to stay here and watch for Seekers. Please just do what I say. Please, I know what happened last time, and I'm sorry, but my job was tons and tons easier."

"Fine, but you better bring them both back, especially Brandon; he needs medical attention, bad!" Rachel said.

"I'll try my best," responded Zak.

"And you bring yourself back," stated Katherine, and she gave him a hug.

"I will," replied Zak as he gave her a kiss goodbye.

Ryan stepped forward. "I'm going with you."

Zak turned to him and replied, "No, I do better alone."

"You don't understand; I've been looking for Brandon for a long time, I was his family's bodyguard."

"What?!" everyone asked.

"Yes, when he was a little boy, his father, George, feared that Kevin would try to kill him and his family again so he hired me. I helped stop Kevin the second time that he tried to kill them, but George wasn't going to let a third time happen, so that's when he decided to move to Banner Village. I would have gone with them, but George thought that since Kevin knew I was their bodyguard from when he tried to attack that I would be with them, so he had me go someplace else as a distraction to capture Kevin. Kevin, on the other hand, must have figured the plan out or had a Seeker listen in, since Brandon's parents ended up being murdered."

"Then why are you still looking for him?" asked Katherine.

"Because they were like a family to me. Brandon was like a son I always wanted. We'd play games, sports, go swim in the lake, fish, hunt, and wrestle. So when I heard the news that his parents had died, I tried my best to get to him, but I was drafted to the army, so I had to go,"

"That's a pretty wild story. All right, let's get moving," announced Zak.

Ryan and Zak were just about to dive. "Do we have everything?" asked Zak.

Then Ryan replied, "I believe so."

"Wait, how are you going to defend yourself against seekers?" Ryan lifted up his arm to reveal a leather brace. He pressed a button and a gun popped up; Ryan grabbed it and a blade flew out the front. "I have a weapon."

"Yea...you do," Zak said, sounding a little jealous. "How does it hold the gun *and* blade?"

"I know a guy. Let's go."

"I've got to get me one of those!" The two dove off the cliff and into the freezing water. Instead of coming up, they swam closer and closer to the other cliff.

They would come up for air as needed. As they expected, the bottom barely had any rocks. It was odd because everywhere else there were rocks. Kevin must have done something to get rid of them.

Ryan took the lead, determined to save the boy he'd taken in. They reached the small land that surround the cliff and took off all the swim gear they had on. Replacing the swimming gear, they put on climbing gear, and Ryan started off first. The two moved quickly and quietly, determined to rescue the other two from Kevin. They scaled the cliff side in about an hour.

Reaching the top, Ryan and Zak both slipped the gear off like a glove. They noticed that there was no way in through the back. The front was the only way, so they started to sneak around the house. While in the back, they noticed that there was a pretty big piece of land there.

Ryan went in through the left and Zak through the right. No Seekers in sight, Ryan scoped the left side out, making sure that the coast was completely clear. As for Zak, he evaluated the house and started for the main entrance.

Once they both reached the front, they tried to quietly open the door and sneak in.

Nothing happened; it was strange, just like at the mansion in Andren. The two were on their toes and ready for anything. Ryan had his gun out and blade in the brace ready to strike anything. Zak had his blade out, getting familiar with his surroundings. The whole house seemed odd. Not even one Seeker, or at least that's what they thought.

⁂

"What! Zak is here! And Ryan? He looks so familiar, and...who is he?"

Brandon was lying on the ground facing the wall. Kevin had Kami chained to a wall.

"Brandon!" whispered Kami. "Brandon, who is this Ryan guy?"

Brandon tried to look at her but just couldn't and whispered back, "I...I don't know."

"If you don't know him and I don't know him, then why would he be coming?"

"Maybe he's just a cop?"

"Ugh, who is he!?" exclaimed Kevin as he walked out of the room.

"What does this Ryan guy look like? Can you see the TV?" asked Brandon.

Kami looked over at the television and whispered, "he has short light brown, almost blonde hair, hazel eyes, and is very muscular."

"He's starting to sound familiar, but I can't put my finger on who he is."

"I've never seen him. How do you know him?"

"I... I'm not sure, I think that he might have done something with or for my father, but why would he be coming?" Brandon then and there fell asleep.

※-※

"Come on, Brandon, hold out for a while. I'll be there soon!" whispered Ryan to himself as he jogged around the house. The house wasn't very big but had its tricks. By pulling on the second light switch on the pad, a floor tile would open up to a storage room, and if he leaned up against a certain spot on the left wall that spot would open up also into a storage room, just like in the movies. Knowing Kevin, his lab had to be behind some secret passage. So Ryan and Zak searched the house from bottom to top pulling on anything that they could find.

As they climbed higher and higher, the less quiet it was in the house. Seekers started to appear, left and right. Zak swung his blade, slicing across the many Seekers. Ryan shot each and every Seeker that crossed his path right in between the eyes. Nothing was going to stop the two.

※

"Get Brandon out there. If they find a way into this lab, I'm doomed, and my plan will fall into ruins!" growled Kevin to a Seeker. The Seeker walked into the cellar, where Brandon and Kami were being held. Brandon was lying on the floor, completely drained of all strength. He now had a broken leg, while Kami was chained to the brick wall, like the many times Brandon was.

The Seeker grabbed Brandon and threw him over his shoulder.

"Tell me where you're taking him!" demanded Kami. The Seeker stopped and looked at her; its red eyes stared at her, almost as if it was trying to put her into a trance. Before the Seeker walked out, Kevin came bursting in through the door.

"I know who he is!"

"Who?" asked Kami.

"That Ryan guy!"

Kami looked up, wanting to know the answer while Kevin explained, with Brandon still unconscious. "This Ryan guy is Brandon's family bodyguard! It seems so strange—an old bodyguard would risk his life to save a pathetic worm like this."

"Shut up! If anyone here is a worm, it's you!"

"Excuse me?"

"You heard me; you're the pathetic worm!"

"You better watch who you're speaking to and what you're saying!"

"No, at least people actually like Brandon, like him enough to risk their lives for him!"

"Shut up or be whipped!" belted Kevin, just as those words were spoken, Kami realized how many times Brandon must have been through this. Inside she knew that he was going to do anything and everything to help her, even if it meant pain for him. "No, you have a chance, right now to stop all this, take it!" Kevin turned around and mumbled something to the Seeker that was holding the unconscious Brandon.

The Seeker nodded and set Brandon down, against the wall. Kevin stood by him and stared. When the Seeker came back in, it was holding a small device. The Seeker gave the device to Kevin and pulled Brandon forward. Kevin then placed the device on the back of Brandon's neck. As soon as the device touched Brandon's skin, all of his wounds, scars, black eye, and everything vanished, and Brandon's eyes flipped open.

※-※

"I hope that they can make it in time," stated Rachel.

"What do you mean 'make it in time'?" asked Katherine.

"Well, you know Kevin. I bet that his plan is to do something to Kami and force Brandon to watch, which will hurt him emotionally, and he'll continue to beat him physically. And after all this—I hope I'm wrong—but won't he kill him?"

"Oh, well... I don't know. I hope not too."

"I want to meet Brandon really bad. He sounds like a cool guy."

"Yea, me too, I just hope that Ryan and Zak get him before he, you know, 'leaves us.'"

"Yea, I can't even imagine what the poor guy went through. I mean after seeing him...how can someone be so sick to even think of doing something like that to someone else!?"

"I know; it's just so horrible!"

The general came walking up from the trail. "Well, I didn't see any Seekers. I don't know about the others, but I bet that they're probably not having any better luck. This just seems strange; I mean, you'd think that he'd have the place crawling with those monsters of his."

"Did you check the miscellaneous objects that are lying around?" responded Rachel.

"Yes, there was nothing." Suddenly behind the general, a breaking tree branch sound occurred and startled the three.

"What was that?" wondered Katherine as she looked around.

"I don't know, a Seeker? But I've never heard of a Seeker that falls out of a tree!" exclaimed Rachel.

"I'll take a look around. I might have just been a village kid playing around in the forest or one of my men," stated the general. He turned around and started to walk toward the broken branch noise.

※

"Have you found anything?" asked Zak quietly.

"No, not yet, but still keep looking. I saw Brandon, and it doesn't look too good," replied Ryan. The two were in a hall pulling on vases and touching every part of every wall. Things were still the same as they were ten minutes ago, nothing new, no new finds, new information, or anything.

"Maybe what the boy thought he saw was nothing. Kevin could be anywhere, in Nelmena, Kili, Fredrena, or on another island. Do you think that there's a chance that the boy lied to us and was working with Kevin?" asked Ryan.

"I don't know. I guess it's a possibility, but before we jump to other conclusions, we need to finish searching here," explained Zak.

"Yea, I know." They searched for a while longer and still found nothing.

"Brandon? Brandon are... are you okay?" Brandon said nothing but walked closer to Kami, holding both of his blades together forming the shape of an X. "Brandon, Brandon please... stop, Brandon!" squirmed Kami, as Brandon walked closer. He was about in the middle of the room now. "Brandon! Brandon, please! Stop! Don't please!" screamed Kami, trying to break free.

"Yes, finally, by the time those idiots get here, it will be too late, and my revenge will have been fulfilled!"

"Brandon! Please!" Brandon had his blades on the wall around her neck. The necklace that she wore was cut and fell to the ground.

She held her breath, hoping that the cold blade wouldn't touch her throat. Kami stared into Brandon's eyes, only to see nothing, nothing at all. She knew that he would do it; he had no control; it was all Kevin. None of this was Brandon. He raised his elbows and went to strike, when they heard a familiar voice speak behind them.

"Brandon, let her go, or Kevin gets it!" threatened Zak.

"If that's Brandon, where are all his scars, cuts, and bruises?" inquired Ryan.

"We don't know, but that's him all right!"

"I applaud you, Zak, and you too, Ryan, but I must say that I'm still not quite sure on who you are or why you're here. But you found the place, and that's very surprising, knowing the intelligence you contain," said Brandon with his usual sarcastic self.

"Be quiet!" Zak sighed out loud, tired of the sarcasm.

"Do it; kill her, and then you go free! Promise!" announced Kevin.

"Don't listen to him. Once you kill her and go free, you, not him, will feel horrible!" warned Zak.

"Come on, Brandon, just drop the blades!" urged Ryan.

"None of you know... I've been waiting for this moment for my entire life; everything I've ever done has been for her, and now... I get something back!" Brandon said, looking down to the floor.

"Please, Brandon, just back away from her, and we can help you!" assured Zak.

"Listen to Zak, Brandon! Please, buddy?" urged Ryan again.

"Fine." He lowered his blades on Kami, and she released her breath in relief. "But if I can't kill her then one of you will take her place!" Brandon threw himself at Zak, who held *his* blade at Kevin's throat.

"Why isn't the general back yet or one of the other men?" wondered Katherine.

"I don't know. He must have..." Rachel tried to come up with something that the general could have been doing, when they heard another breaking branch noise.

"I don't think that those are the kids?!" stated Katherine as she backed away, behind Rachel.

"Me neither," agreed Rachel, as she backed away too. Suddenly the trees around them started to rustle, and tons of little gleaming red eyes showed all around them.

"Oh my gosh, th-the Seekers. They must have killed the general and the others!" yelled Rachel. Just then all the Seekers climbed out of the trees, down the trunks. The two drew their weapons and were ready, hopefully, for whatever had to happen.

Meanwhile, back at the lab, Brandon swung his blade down at Zak from above and swung at Ryan from the left. Ryan didn't want to shoot the boy he took in as his son or stab him either, so all he could really do was defend with the blade he had. Same with Zak. Brandon was coming at them with full force, leading them out of the lab. Zak was forced to leave Kevin back in the cell with Kami, and he knew that it wasn't the best thing he could have done. Zak, in a duel lock with Brandon, threw Brandon's blades back at him and tried to get him in the side and nailed him sharply. As they battled, Kami was set free by Kevin, he hoped that when she went out to the three guys, Brandon would see her and kill her. She picked up her necklace, and she ran to where the three were fighting.

※

Rachel and Katherine were surrounded and battling all the many Seekers. Katherine threw a few daggers and swung at some; as for Rachel, she had both ends of her spear out, using them at any chance given to her. Rachel kicked one Seeker down and stabbed it in the chest. Katherine slid behind another and threw her blade in its back. All the Seekers now had their nails fully out, scratching both girls on their arms and backs. Even though they were feeling the pain, they knew that they couldn't stop, not even for a second, or else it would cost them their lives.

※

Once Kami reached the three guys, she started to give some helpful information "Zak! Ryan! Aim for the back of his neck! There's a device; that's the thing that's controlling him!"

Holding Brandon back, Zak turned to her and replied, "What? On the back of the neck?"

"Yes, that's the only thing that will stop him, and whatever you do, don't hurt him!"

"Won't he just heal? Like last time?"

"With the device on, yes!" Zak shoved Brandon back and ran toward Kami, leaving Brandon to Ryan.

"What are you talking about?" questioned Zak.

"That device is the thing that heals him, but as soon

as it unlatches from his neck, everything appears, including the hits he received from the battle!"

Zak rolled his head around along with his eyes in irritation. "This is so messed up!" He turned back to help Ryan, who had Brandon backed in a corner.

Struggling to hold Brandon there, Ryan turned to Zak who was standing next to him. "What now?"

Zak went to move Brandon's head down, but Brandon refused and kicked Zak back a little. Brandon also tried to kick Ryan from below and succeeded. Now free, Brandon turned toward a wall and ran over to it. Ryan and Zak looked at each other wondering why he wouldn't just run up through the entrance, but when they looked back at Brandon, they saw him hold a brick down, opening the wall behind him.

※-※

Finishing off a Seeker or two, Katherine looked at Rachel, who was holding back one of the clawing beasts. "What now? We can't just stay here; they're multiplying! We can't hold out forever!"

Rachel looked back at her and nodded then shoved the Seeker back. "Should we jump?"

"Do you know if a shore is down there?" Rachel went to look as Katherine defended her.

"No close shore; but Seekers, I don't think, do well in water, so let's do it!" The two killed the last Seeker in their way and leaped off the cliff into the cold water below.

When they looked up, back to the cliff Kevin was on, they saw in the back three figures, doing what seemed to be battling. "Oh no, Brandon is fighting Zak and Ryan!" worried Rachel,

"If there's anything I know about Zak, it's he's *not* leaving without Brandon...alive," assured Katherine.

⁂

Brandon stopped and swung his blade around him, to keep the other two away from him. "Get out of here!" barked Brandon.

"I'm not leaving without you; I've been searching for you almost all my life! And now that I've finally found you, I'm not going to just forget about you and leave!" replied Ryan with his gun pointed up at Brandon, just to warn him.

Ryan stepped forward, and Brandon backed up with each step Ryan made. Zak stared at Brandon, thinking of a way to get the device off. Brandon ran after Ryan. Ryan dropped the gun and used the blade he had. Zak came from behind and pulled Brandon away, forcing Brandon to drop his blades. "Get the device off his neck!" Zak struggled, and Brandon squirmed to get free, while Ryan searched on the back of Brandon's neck.

"I don't see it!"

"What?"

"There's nothing here!"

"Keep checking." Brandon started to get free, and Zak tried harder to hold him in place "Check again...and fast!" Ryan searched and searched then went to check in the hairline.

"How small is the device?" asked Ryan, panicking a little.

"I don't know, but once you find it, yank it off!"

Just then Brandon broke free and ran for the edge of the cliff. He stopped and looked at Ryan, shaking his head. "You've wasted your life!" then he turned and jumped.

Ryan, revealing a look of anger, ran full speed to the cliff, and dove after Brandon. A little behind, Ryan held his arms at his sides and feet together, gaining speed, just about to catch up to Brandon. He caught up and grabbed him; Brandon struggled around and punched Ryan across the face. Countering, Ryan kneed Brandon in the gut; Brandon strained for a breath and flipped Ryan from the side to below him. Ryan crunched into a ball and placed his feet on Brandon's chest, pushing Brandon away. Brandon let the wind carry him away as they hit water.

Once Ryan floated to the surface, he looked around and didn't see Brandon. Ryan started to cry out, "Brandon! Brandon, where are you?! Answer me!" When there was no reply, Ryan knew that Brandon must have still been under the water. Diving back under, Ryan searched frantically for him, but he was nowhere in sight. He could have been anywhere since the wind carried him off and the waves were strong. Ryan came back up for air then went back down; he looked below in all directions toward the bottom until he finally saw him sinking, unconscious.

Ryan viciously fought against the current, and grabbed Brandon, who was now beaten and scarred. Pulling Brandon to the surface, Ryan noticed that he was fifty times lighter than he should have been. Getting Brandon to the top was the easy part, now he had to swim to shore. Even though Brandon was lighter, swimming with two people, one being unconscious, just wasn't easy especially with waves as big and strong as they were.

Ryan sunk a few times, here and there, but always kept Brandon up above the water. Once they reached the mini piece of land that surrounded the cliff, Ryan laid Brandon down and checked to see if he was breathing. Zak, flipping his wet hair around, jogged up beside Ryan.

"Is he breathing?"

Ryan waited a minute before answering then replied with worry. "No, he's not!"

"Man!" They heard a loud splash from behind and turned to see what was coming out of the water. It was Kami. When she reached Brandon, nothing had changed; he was dying and only a miracle could save his life. Kami instantly began CPR. She repeatedly whispered, "Come on Brandon, come on, you can do this, please." Brandon balanced on the brink of death.

21

Zak had called in a chopper to transport Ryan and Brandon to the nearest hospital. Kami stayed with Zak, allowing Ryan to accompany the man who was like a son to him. When they arrived, the doctors immediately sent Brandon to have surgery. Things weren't looking good, not one bit.

After the surgery, and the nurses finding Brandon a room, the doctor walked up to Ryan holding a clipboard. He didn't look like he bore any good news. "You're Brandon's guardian, correct?"

"I guess you could say that. How is he?"

"Well." The doc set the clipboard down and continued. "I'm going to be very straightforward with you. Brandon isn't in the best condition, and he could die within twelve hours. He's lost way too much blood; he has a broken leg, pneumonia, and infected cuts including deep ones. He's not at a healthy weight, not at all. He has three broken ribs, a dislocated shoulder, third-degree burns all over, and stitches in his arm from, what I'm told was a dagger. His heartbeat is slowing down, and blood is having a hard time moving throughout the body.

His heart is seriously struggling. Both eyes are black. His lungs are weaker, so he has a hard time breathing. He could possibly fall into a coma, and just so many more things."

"Is there any good news?"

"Just a little, we have been able to stop the bleeding on certain cuts."

"That's it?"

"Yes, I'm terribly sorry."

Ryan looked to the floor, in shock at the news. "Is there any paperwork that has to be filled out?"

"Yes, what is Brandon's full name?"

"Brandon Ray Teonen."

Once all the paperwork had been filled out, Ryan decided to visit Brandon. The room was dark, due to the blinds being shut. Brandon lay still in the bed, hooked up to a heart monitor, an oxygen tank, and other systems that Ryan had never seen before. His leg positioned up in the air above his heart, he was wrapped in gauze on certain places and bare on others, and he had been tucked in with four heavy blankets. He looked worse than he could imagine. Ryan pulled up a chair next to Brandon's bed. "Hey, it's been a while since I've seen you." He tried to smile but couldn't. "I've searched my entire life for you, and now that I've found you, you're gonna leave me again."

Brandon's breathing was heavy and deep, the heart monitor went at a slower than normal pace. Ryan's eyes started to turn red as water built up on his bottom eyelid. "I only wish that I could have been there with you at that village. I-I didn't mean to leave you." He paused a second to breath. "This is all my fault. If I wouldn't have left you, believing Kevin would follow me none of this would have happened, and you would still be able to live. You wouldn't have gone through all you did. You wouldn't have had to suffer."

※-※

Each hour Ryan would check on Brandon, hoping with all his heart that some miracle would happen. Nothing changed. Kami and the others wouldn't be able to make it to the hospital in time. If they were to show, he'd be gone. It was only a matter of time.

Two more hours till the doctors predicted time expired, Ryan sat in Brandon's room, by his bed when suddenly the heart monitor went flat. Brandon's heart stopped, and the time had come. Ryan jumped up and flew out the door to grab a doctor. The doctor grabbed the supplies he needed and tore to Brandon's room. They busted through the door, doctors, nurses, and equipment.

"Excuse me, but you're going to need to stay out here," said one of the many nurses.

"No, that's my son! Let me in!"

"I'm sorry, but you have to stay out here."

"Fine." Ryan sat nervously on a chair outside the room scared for his "son."

"Clear," announced one of the nurses. The doctor nodded and zapped Brandon's chest. His body hopped into the air then flew back down. Nothing. "Clear," continued the nurse, and the doctor did the same thing. Still nothing.

"Take it up." The nurse did what she was told, and the doctor zapped away. Once again, nothing. They increased the charges over and over.

They continued the process for a little while until they clumped out of the room. Everyone looked gloomy and depressed, which wasn't a good sign. Automatically Ryan believed and knew in his heart that Brandon had died.

The main doctor walked out, and Ryan went up to him, just wanting to get the news over with, asking, "How is he?"

The doctor took in a deep breath in then blew out. "You prayed for a miracle...and God gave it to him." Ryan sighed in relief, thanking God with all he had.

"Thank you, thank you so much," thanked Ryan.

"Well, he's still on the brink and still has a chance of death, so keep praying."

"It's still better than actually having him dead."

"Oh, and the scientists that were studying the device found some very interesting information. They found that the device was the one thing that kept him alive during his time with Kevin, since the device healed him. It held in all the blood and healed everything just like nothing happened. We propose that we put the device on him right now and have it heal him until his actual body fully recovers, but the problem with that is, well, we don't know where Kevin is or if he could still take control."

"Is there a guarantee that if the device is put on him that he will be healed?"

"That's what we believe."

"How long would the device have to be on him?"

"Well… we're not really sure on that… Considering the condition that he's in… I don't know."

"Alright, let's hook it on him, but if something starts to happen, then I'll hold him back and someone needs to pull the device off."

"Alright, but I'm warning you that he still may be able to transport."

"That's a chance that I'm willing to take."

22

Ryan stood in place, holding Brandon when a thought crossed his mind. He looked up at the doctor. "Why don't we just keep Zak and the others at the house in the lab when the device is placed on? That way we can make sure Brandon stays under our control."

The doctor nodded. "Yea, I think something like that should be able to work. But wasn't Kevin's original hideout with Brandon at the mansion, the one here in Andren?"

"Yes, he ended up moving, since he knew that Zak and the others were coming…"

"So wouldn't he have a control station there?"

"Maybe."

"I'll call a team of police to be placed there."

"All right, but hurry, we don't know how long he's going to last."

Zak turned around to go back to the house at Banner Village as a team headed for the mansion. While all this happened, Ryan stayed with Brandon, who still wasn't doing real well. "You're gonna be better soon." Brandon breathed in, keeping it in for a couple seconds then released the air. His heartbeats were slow but steady. He barely looked human, even though they cleaned all the dirt, mud, and blood off him.

The doctor walked in. "All right, we're set. Are you sure you want to try this?"

Ryan nodded. "Yea."

Once again, everyone stood in their positions. Ryan held Brandon by the shoulders as the doctor placed the device on Brandon's flesh. As soon as the device latched onto his skin, all the scars, burns, cuts, whip marks, and everything dissolved into his skin. Brandon's eyes flipped open, to him, all the things that surrounded him were black and blurry.

"Pl-please d-don't send me! Please!" Brandon cried out scared to death as he thrashed around like a wild beast. Ryan held him down.

"Brandon! Brandon, it's me. It's me, Ryan, remember?"

"No! No, I don't know you. You're-you're just a Seeker!"

"I was your family's bodyguard! Now calm down." Brandon declined the order and tried with all his might to get free.

"I won't hurt them! You're not getting me to hurt any of them!"

"I don't want you to hurt anyone! I'm not Kevin or a Seeker! It's really me!" Brandon had some strength to him, and keeping him back wasn't the easiest task. "Brandon! Chill out! Just stop and look, look at me in the eyes, and you'll see, it's me!"

Brandon stopped and breathed heavily, looking

deeply into his eyes; there resided a soul. "You're...you're not a seeker, but I still don't know you."

"Your father was being tracked down and Kevin tried to kill him, so he hired me to protect you, your mom, and dad."

"R-Ryan? I think I know you now. We used to wrestle all the time, and...and you'd always let me win..."

"Yes. Do you remember now?"

"Sort of, but if you were our bodyguard, why are my parents dead?"

"Your father sent me to another place to distract Kevin, but he didn't fall for the trick. And when I heard the news, I tried to get to you, but I was drafted to the army."

"You'd always tell me to not be afraid, that you'd protect me..."

"Yes." Ryan nodded. "Yes, I would say that."

"You were more of a father to me than a bodyguard, more of a father than my own dad." Ryan smiled as Brandon finished the words. The two swung their arms around each other.

Ryan helped Brandon out of the hospital bed. He held on to Ryan for a second then stood on his own. "How? How is this happening?"

"What do mean?"

"How am I me, when everything's gone?"

"The device healed you, and people are at the stations Kevin controlled you with."

"Are you sure that this will help?"

"Do you want a lie or the truth?"

"Alright, I get it. You're not sure." The two walked around the hospital for a bit. Brandon had trouble walking on his own in the beginning, since he hadn't walked on his own for almost a year, but sooner or later he learned and was up walking like he'd been doing it each and every day.

Later that night, the doctor wanted to see Brandon's progress on his real body. So they removed the device, his real body still remained in a fatal stage. The doctor placed the device back on Brandon's neck while Ryan began talking with him.

"What would happen if the control centers were destroyed?" asked Ryan.

"I'm not sure," answered Brandon.

"Would the device continue to work?" Ryan wondered.

"I don't know. Should we *try* and destroy them?"

"Well, yea, you don't want to have to worry about being controlled?"

"Yea, but... what is my body like when the device is off?"

"It's not so good, why?"

"Would I die if this device isn't on me?"

"It's a possibility, why?"

"Just thinking about if we should give it a try."

"All right, but if you don't want them destroyed, then they won't be."

※-※

Ryan, Zak, and the others stood outside Brandon's room talking, since Brandon was sleeping. "How did you guys get here so fast?" asked Ryan.

"Through a blur," replied Zak. "We figured that, instead taking forever to drive, why not make it quick and easy?"

"Nice."

"How is Brandon?" wondered Kami.

"Actually he's doing really good. Like I said over the computer, we put the device on him, and now he's doing great."

"So his real body, how is that one?"

"Same, it's actually doing pretty good, it's still not in the best condition, but it's doing better than when we first came here."

"That's good; we smashed the center like you told us."

"Good, so did the cops at the mansion, and the device still works."

"I wonder how?"

"Me too."

§~§

Morning hit, Brandon woke up slowly, the device still latched onto his neck. He stretched out his legs and arms then went to get out of bed. He walked over to the chair in the far right corner and grabbed his shirt, slipping it on. Brandon had no idea that Zak, Kami, Rachel, and Katherine were all here, so he opened the door and slipped out. He wandered the halls for bit, just to wake up, then headed to the hospital cafeteria.

Meanwhile, Ryan and all the others finished and left the cafeteria, just as Brandon walked in. They all piled next to Brandon's door; Ryan peeked in to see if Brandon was still sleeping. When he did he didn't see Brandon; he fully opened the door and saw that Brandon's shirt wasn't on the chair. Kami walked over to Ryan and calmly asked, "Where is he?"

Ryan looked at her. "Don't worry; he's probably walking around to wake himself up. He does it almost every day. He might even be in the cafeteria."

Brandon finished his breakfast and walked around the halls just as Ryan and the others walked back in. They looked around but didn't see him; in the meantime, Brandon reached his room. Since he had four heavier blankets on the bed and the air conditioning wouldn't kick on, Brandon took off his shirt, threw it on the chair, grabbed the remote, and hopped into bed. As for the others, since they didn't see him anywhere, they decided to head back to the room, but once they reached it, they saw that a doctor and nurses were heading in to check up on Brandon's real body. Just as the door was about to shut, Kami peeked in; she saw Brandon speaking with the doctor, then out of the corner of his eye he saw Kami.

"Kami? Kami!" Brandon went for the door, but the doctor pulled him back.

"You need to stay here, then after I'm done you can go see them."

"No, no, I want to see them now." Brandon jerked forward, but as he did the doctor pulled the device off, and he fell back into the doctor's arms. The doctor laid him down and took his notes on Brandon's condition. Before placing the device back onto Brandon's neck, the doctor walked out of the room and explained his real condition.

"Do you want the good news or the bad news?"

Kami looked at him. "Good."

"Well, he's not on the brink anymore." Everyone

sighed with relief, but the bad news was yet to come. "The bad news is that he still has all the things he did before, with some being healed. Also he's came down with this disease. We still don't know how he contracted it, but it's very rare, and we haven't found a cure for it. It's called the evanitis syndrome. It is a virus that effects the emotions. The evanitis syndrome will change his emotions rapidly, mostly to the emotion opposite of what he normally is, but then stop and leave him normal. It also leaves the patient with temporary memory loss of what happened when he was in the opposite emotion. Like if the patient went on a rampage and said some things then went back to normal, he wouldn't remember what he said. But what most people do remember is that they have the disease, and they know and feel when the random emotions will kick in. It isn't contagious, but can be very dangerous. Little words could set him off like a cannon, depending on the kind of guy he is."

"What do you mean by that?" questioned Kami.

"Well, what is his typical emotion?"

"Kind of laid back and protective."

"Well, from what we've seen on others, the opposite emotions are what come out, so he'd be very uptight and aggressive."

Kami took in a calming breath of air. "The disease won't be there when the device is on, right?"

"I'm afraid that it will, but it won't show for another few years."

"Why a few years? And how can you tell that he has the disease before it even shows?" queried Ryan.

"Well, this disease forms very slowly. It's not painful to him, but to the people around him, it is very hurtful.

We can tell he has it because in his blood we can see signs of it starting. While the disease is still forming, it attaches itself to the side of the blood vein and it won't move with the blood, but once it's fully developed, the disease will unlatch from the vein, so the blood carries it throughout the body, allowing it to show the effects. But sometimes little particles get mixed in with the blood and are carried along with it, and that's what happened to Brandon. Fortunately, though, when this happened, we were drawing blood to be tested and the particles were caught in the tube."

"How long do you believe it will take for this virus to develop?"

"Hard to say, but my guess would be between four to seven years."

The doctor finally allowed people to go in, but instead of everyone going in, they thought that Kami should have a little alone time with him. Kami walked in the room and sat on the chair beside Brandon's bed as a nurse placed the device on the back of his neck. Brandon's eyes opened to see Kami. Noticing that he had awakened, Kami jumped up. Her hand was in a fist with the other hand on top underneath her chin.

"Brandon!" Her eyes started to tear up, Brandon sat up.

"Kami? Is that really you?"

"Yes! Yes, it's me!"

He smiled. "Come here." He grabbed her arm, pulled her next to him and kissed her. "I've missed you so much!"

"I know; I've missed you too," she whispered.

Brandon examined her. "Are you alright? Did I hurt you in any way while—"

Kami interrupted him. "I'm fine, but you're the one I should be asking questions to. How do you feel? Are you okay? Is there anything I can do? The doctor already told me about your real body's condition. I can only imagine what you went through."

Brandon smiled "I'm fine,"

"Oh Brandon, I was so worried. I'm sorry for not getting there sooner I—"

"Kami, it's okay. Really. I'm glad you showed up when you did. And thank you for coming after me." He touched her hand as tears ran down her cheeks.

"You know I think God had us go through all that for one purpose," he whispered as his lips touched hers.

"Is that so? What's the one purpose?"

The two continued to kiss for a second until Brandon answered, "To tell Kevin how to be saved."

Kami smiled. "You know, I'm so amazed how you can go through all that you did and still care for the man that did it to you."

"It's like Job. He loved and praised God and received all that he could ever want, but when the devil said that he only praised God because he had all the stuff he did, God allowed it all to be taken away, his herds of sheep and cattle, money, servants, house, and even his family just to show that Job still loved and praised God."

"That is truly amazing... Oh and I just thought of another purpose." Brandon looked at her.

"What?"

"God put us through all that to give us time alone so you could tell me about that tiger," she joked. Brandon laughed, and they kissed once again.

You can invite Jesus Christ into your heart today to become your personal Lord and Savior. It is our earnest prayer that you accept your gift of salvation today. He is ready and waiting to hear from you!

"That if thou shalt confess with thy mouth the Lord Jesus, and shalt believe in thine heart that God hath raised him from the dead, thou shalt be saved" (Romans 10:9).

1: Admit you are a sinner. See Romans 3:10.

2: Be willing to turn from sin (repent). See Acts 17:30.

3: Believe that Jesus Christ died for you, was buried and rose from the dead. See Romans 10:9–10.

4: Through prayer, invite Jesus into your life to become your personal Lord and Savior. See Romans 10:13.

What to pray:

Dear God, I am a sinner and need forgiveness. I believe that Jesus Christ shed his precious blood and died for my sin. I am willing to turn from the sin. I now invite Christ to come into my heart and life as my personal Savior.